THE FORTUNES OF TEXAS

*Follow the lives and loves of a complex family
with a rich history and deep ties
in the Lone Star State.*

THE WEDDING GIFT

The town of Rambling Rose, Texas,
is brimming with excitement over the
upcoming wedding of five Fortune couples!
They're scheduled to tie the knot on
New Year's Eve, but one wedding gift
arrives early, setting off a mystery
that could send shock waves through the
entire Fortune family...

Financial adviser Beau Fortune
was born into wealth; Sofia De Leon grew up
poor and built her own successful business
from scratch. When both are nominated for the
Lone Star Best Award, it's game on for Sofia,
who considers Beau the enemy.
But that doesn't stop the sparks from flying
when the two are forced to work together...

Dear Reader,

If you're like me—a big Fortunes of Texas fan—you can hardly wait for the January Harlequin Special Edition novels to release so you can read the first book in the new series. Over the years, I've been fortunate to have taken part in over ten of the amazing series and have worked with many great authors to bring these stories to life. And this year was no different.

In *Anyone But a Fortune*, the characters' goals, motivations and conflicts were different than most of the books I've written. I mean, who can turn down a drop-dead gorgeous man who is also bright, personable and wealthy? Well, Beau Fortune is all that and more.

When Beau meets Sofia De Leon, a Tejano businesswoman who is as beautiful as she is brilliant, he is instantly attracted to her. But Sofia grew up poor and had to work hard for everything she's accomplished. She's not about to fall for the charms of a man whose family has given him every advantage—and continues to do so. Just his last name affords him opportunities others don't have. And when they learn they are both nominated for the same award, the battle is on!

I hope you enjoy reading this book as much as I enjoyed writing it!

Happy reading!

Judy

PS: I love hearing from my readers. You can contact me through my website, judyduarte.com, or on Facebook, Facebook.com/judyduartenovelist. And if you're a fan of Western romances, check out Wild for Westerns from Harlequin, a Facebook page where many of my Harlequin author friends hang out: Facebook.com/groups/290667098916318.

Anyone But a Fortune

JUDY DUARTE

HARLEQUIN

SPECIAL
EDITION

If you purchased this book without a cover you should be aware
that this book is stolen property. It was reported as "unsold and
destroyed" to the publisher, and neither the author nor the
publisher has received any payment for this "stripped book."

Special thanks and acknowledgment are given
to Judy Duarte for her contribution to
The Fortunes of Texas: The Wedding Gift miniseries.

HARLEQUIN®

SPECIAL EDITION™

Recycling programs
for this product may
not exist in your area.

ISBN-13: 978-1-335-40839-6

Anyone But a Fortune

Copyright © 2022 by Harlequin Books S.A.

All rights reserved. No part of this book may be used or reproduced in
any manner whatsoever without written permission except in the case of
brief quotations embodied in critical articles and reviews.

This is a work of fiction. Names, characters, places and incidents
are either the product of the author's imagination or are used fictitiously.
Any resemblance to actual persons, living or dead, businesses,
companies, events or locales is entirely coincidental.

This edition published by arrangement with Harlequin Books S.A.

For questions and comments about the quality of this book,
please contact us at CustomerService@Harlequin.com.

Harlequin Enterprises ULC
22 Adelaide St. West, 41st Floor
Toronto, Ontario M5H 4E3, Canada
www.Harlequin.com

Printed in U.S.A.

Since 2002, *USA TODAY* bestselling author **Judy Duarte** has written over forty books for Harlequin Special Edition, earned two RITA® Award nominations, won two Maggie Awards and received a National Readers' Choice Award. When she's not cooped up in her writing cave, she enjoys traveling with her husband and spending quality time with her grandchildren. You can learn more about Judy and her books on her website, judyduarte.com, or at Facebook.com/judyduartenovelist.

Books by Judy Duarte

Harlequin Special Edition

Rancho Esperanza

Starting Over with the Sheriff
Their Night to Remember
A Secret Between Us

The Fortunes of Texas: The Wedding Gift

Anyone But a Fortune

The Fortunes of Texas: Rambling Rose

The Mayor's Secret Fortune

The Fortunes of Texas: All Fortune's Children

Wed by Fortune

Visit the Author Profile page
at Harlequin.com for more titles.

To Jeanne M. Dickson, a talented author
who helped me and my muse through a difficult year
and who encouraged me to never give up.
Thanks for being only a text or phone call away.

Chapter One

A light breeze rustled the trees as Beau Fortune headed toward the Rambling Rose Dog Park, his grip tight on the leash tethered to a happy-go-lucky shepherd mix. He'd rather be running along the bike trail up ahead, but at least, his biceps were getting a workout, thanks to the strength and energy of his neighbor's nine-month-old rescue.

Beau liked animals well enough, but it had never seemed the right time to bring a pet into his life. That's why he didn't mind looking after M.P., Dan Gallagher's overgrown pup. Dan's wife had passed away six months ago, and he'd told Beau that though he kept busy during the day, the evenings often dragged on, long and lonely. Beau had suggested that he get a pet, and damned if Dan didn't jump on that idea.

An Army vet who'd been part of the military police, Dan had dubbed his new dog M.P. But what a misnomer. Following rules and obeying his master didn't come easy for the goofy mutt. Still, he was likable. There was an innocent sweetness about him, much like a well-meaning but impulsive child.

M.P. stopped to sniff a small shrub along the pathway, so Beau took a moment to shrug his shoulders a couple of times in an attempt to work out the knot that had grown tight during a trying day at Fortune Investments.

A bird chirped in a nearby maple, and the cool breeze kicked up a notch. It was good to be outdoors this afternoon. There was nothing he needed more than some fresh air and a relaxing walk that would allow him to leave a stressful day behind.

M.P. barked at the chirping bird, then tugged hard at the leash. So much for expecting to have a leisurely stroll in the park.

"Settle down. You're no bird dog." Beau pulled back on the leash just as his cell phone rang.

It was probably Draper, his brother, who was also his business partner and housemate. Draper hadn't been happy about the surprise meeting their father had sprung on them this afternoon. Those video conference calls with the home office could be long and dreary, but Draper had agreed to stay and let Beau cut out early as long as he took M.P. with him.

Draper hadn't objected to having Dan's dog at the house or at the office, since the Fortune brothers had been trying to create a sense of belonging in their new community. And that meant being good neighbors.

As Beau pulled the smartphone out of his back pocket, M.P. lunged forward again, this time hard enough to loosen Beau's grip on the leash and the phone. The latter landed facedown in the dirt.

"Crap." Beau stooped to grab it just as M.P. let out a yip and sprang ahead. The leash slipped free of Beau's fingers, and the rascally mutt took off like a shot, loping across the park. He appeared to be heading toward a woman and a fluffy white dog with a red banana tied around its neck. The woman spun a blue plastic disc into the air, and her talented pet took off after it, leaping up and making a great catch. Then, while holding the disc in its teeth, it trotted back to its owner.

Apparently, M.P. wanted to get in on the doggie fun and games. Beau cursed under his breath and declined the call before he had a lawsuit on his hands.

"Come back here," he called out, but M.P. continued to run forward, his tail wagging like mad. "Crazy mutt."

The Frisbee-flying woman quickly reached for her smaller dog, lifting it into her arms to protect it. Too bad she didn't realize that M.P. was all yip and no bite.

"Don't worry," he called out to the attractive, dark-haired woman who was wearing a pair of black yoga pants and a red top. "M.P.'s too friendly and way too energetic, but he wouldn't hurt a flea—and certainly not your dog. Or you."

He continued his approach, but when her big brown eyes met his, recognition slammed into him and he damn near froze in his tracks.

It was *her*. The stunning brunette he'd met last month at the Valentine's Day party at the Hotel Fortune. She'd been rocking a sexy red dress, and he'd been instantly drawn to her. Unlike Draper, who didn't have a problem approaching an attractive woman he'd like to get to know, Beau tended to be more reserved. But he hadn't been that night. He'd thrown back the last of his first glass of merlot, then crossed the dance floor, intent on introducing himself.

He'd barely said hello and managed a little small talk when a tall, slender man interrupted them and gave Beau a cold, threatening stare. Beau had immediately backed off. Not that he'd been intimidated. He just didn't like public drama.

Now, as luck would have it and thanks to M.P.'s overly friendly nature, he had an opportunity to approach her again.

"Sorry about that." He snatched the leash off the grass and pulled the dog back into some degree of submission as he straightened. "You may not remember me, but we met. Sort of."

Her brow lifted, and a grin tugged at her pink-glossed lips. "Actually, I *do* remember you."

Before he could come up with a clever response, an odd expression crossed her face and she flushed as if he'd caught her doing something unexpected or inappropriate. But she quickly recovered and offered him a full-blown smile that kicked up his heart rate and warmed his blood.

"It was on Valentine's Day. At the Hotel Fortune." She studied M.P. for a moment, clearly concluding that he wasn't a threat to anyone. Her white fur baby had come to the same conclusion, because it began to squirm in her arms, clearly wanting to get down.

Beau cleared his throat. "I'm sorry about M.P.'s interference. He means well, but he's a rescue and still learning his manners."

She glanced at the fluffy dog in her arms. "This is Pepe. He's a rescue, too." Then she placed Pepe on the grass, where the two dogs began the let's-sniff-each-other-and-make-friends routine, making an unexpected meet-and-greet look easy.

"Impy is a good name for him," she said. "I can see he's a bit mischievous."

"He definitely has an impish side, but his name is actually in reference to the military police. His owner was in the service." Beau glanced down at M.P. "He isn't mine, though. I'm dog sitting for my neighbor." He nodded toward Pepe, who appeared to have a little spaniel in its family pedigree. "Do you two come here often?"

"I try to. I work crazy hours, so I like to spend as much of my free time with Pepe as I can. In fact, I have a dog sitter, too. Two of them, actually. My mom and my grandmother." She nodded to the right, toward a small neighborhood of Spanish-style, white stucco condominiums with red brick roofs. "They live in that complex over there and keep him when I'm at work or away from home."

"Sounds like the perfect setup."

"It works for us."

They'd just spoken longer to each other this afternoon than they had at the party, yet he knew more about her dog and her family than he did her. "We never got a chance to exchange names that night. Mine's Beau. And yours…?"

She paused for a moment as if she wasn't sure whether to offer him an imaginary moniker or her real name. "It's Sofia."

He decided she'd given him an honest answer, because the name suited her. She had a striking look about her, with an olive complexion, high cheekbones, a slender nose and full, kissable lips.

She also had a figure that was curved to perfection. Damn, she was attractive. Too bad she was taken.

Or was she?

"I, uh…" He cleared his throat. "I didn't mean to upset your boyfriend at the party."

"You didn't do anything wrong. He'd jumped to conclusions, and I set him straight."

She made it sound simple, but there had to be more going on than that. Beau hadn't been able to keep his eyes off her the rest of the night, and he'd noted the tension in her stance and the serious expression she'd worn. She hadn't been happy, and the boyfriend had been clearly pissed about something.

Beau hoped it hadn't been him. He probably ought to let the subject drop, but he shrugged. "Even so, I'm sorry if I created any problems for you."

She tucked a long strand of dark hair behind her ear, revealing a diamond stud and a lovely neck. "There isn't any need to apologize. In the long run, you did me a favor."

At that, Beau's interest piqued and his attraction stirred. "I did? How so?"

She paused for a couple of beats. "Let's just say

relationships are complicated. And some aren't supposed to last."

Aw. So they broke up.

Before Beau could say a word, his cell phone rang. It was probably Draper again. And since the call could be important, he shouldn't let it roll over to voice mail. "I'm sorry, Sofia. I don't want to be rude, but I need to take this."

As he reached into his back pocket to retrieve the phone, she said, "No problem. Go ahead. I need to go."

His cell continued to ring, but he couldn't let her walk away like that. "Wait a minute."

She turned to face him, and her gaze locked on his. "Yes?"

"Do you come here often?"

"Almost daily."

"About this same time?"

She nodded, then pointed at the ringing smart-phone in his hand. "You're going to lose that call."

He tossed her a grin. "Then, maybe I'll see you tomorrow."

She returned his smile. "Maybe you will."

He certainly hoped so. At least, he knew where to find her.

"Come on, Pepe." She snapped her fingers, and as she headed toward the bike path, the dog pranced along beside her, following her lead, even without a leash.

Beau swiped his finger across the screen, then pressed the phone to his ear. "I'm sorry I missed your call, bro. How'd that meeting go? Just the usual monthly update?"

"Yes, but there's a problem. The website crashed."

"Uh-oh. Did we get hacked?"

"No, there isn't any evidence of that. Looks like it's a bug in the app. The tech guys are working on it. They hope to get it up and running again soon."

"Good." Beau glanced over his shoulder and spotted Sofia and her dog nearing the bike path.

M.P. let out a whine, clearly unhappy to see his new friend leaving. Beau knew how he felt.

"But I do have some good news," Draper added. "I just got word that Fortune Investments was nominated for a Lone Star Best Award."

At that, Beau's focus returned to the call. "No kidding?" The Lone Star Best was a prestigious award given to the movers and shakers in various industries in the state, not just finance. "That's *great* news."

"I agree. People have really begun to take notice of us." Draper sounded as excited as a Little Leaguer who'd just hit a walk-off grand slam. "They invited us to a luncheon on Friday in Austin for the nominees. The next round is some kind of community competition—whatever that means.

We'll get further instructions then. Are you free on Friday?"

"Yeah, even if I have to reschedule things. How about you?"

"Not really," Draper said. "Belle has already asked me for the day off, and I told her it was okay."

Their sister had been working as their office manager, although she planned to start her own retail business in the near future.

"Did she tell you why she wanted the time off?" Beau asked.

"She and Jack are checking out a few properties that might be suitable for her boutique. So why don't you go and represent Fortune Investments? I'll hold down the fort at the office."

"We both ought to attend. I'd suggest that we call a temp service and get someone to come in and answer phones."

"You know Belle does a hell of a lot more than just answer the phones. And there's a lot going on at the office now. I'll cover for Belle. Besides, I have plans to go out of town this weekend. I'm flying to Vegas, and I don't want to get tied up in Austin and risk missing my flight."

Beau slowly shook his head, a grin tugging at his lips. Draper had always been able to manipulate things in his own favor. "Looks like I drew the short straw. Again."

"Don't look at it that way. That nomination is an honor. And you'll make Fortune Investments look good."

Draper was right. The home office was in New Orleans, and the two brothers had recently opened a branch in Rambling Rose. The recognition was going to provide them with valuable promotion.

"All right," Beau said. "I'll go on my own. Text me the details, and I'll get it on my calendar."

Once the call ended, he glanced down at M.P., who was looking up at him with sad, puppy-dog eyes that said he wasn't happy to lose his new friend.

"Yeah, I hear you, buddy." Beau took one last look at the bike path Sofia and her dog had taken just moments ago. She was out of sight now, but that didn't mean he wouldn't see her again.

And if all went as planned, their next meeting would be tomorrow afternoon.

You may not remember me...

Sofia De Leon certainly had remembered him. The tall, dark-haired stranger had approached her at the party and tossed her a charming smile that nearly stole her breath away. From the first moment he said hello, he'd kind of reminded her of Cary Grant, or another of those polished 1940s movie stars. She'd found him both handsome and charming.

If truth be told, she'd felt more than a stir of attraction that evening. But at the time, she'd been committed to Patrick, so she wouldn't have pursued anything.

Apparently, Patrick didn't know her well enough to realize that, because when he interrupted them, he immediately gave Beau a death stare, and Beau had gracefully sauntered away. Patrick accused her of hooking up with another man while she was on a date with him, which she'd never do.

Since Sofia hadn't even learned Beau's name at that point, she didn't think she'd ever see him again. So, needless to say, running into him at the dog park had taken her by complete surprise. Amazingly enough, she found him just as appealing in a casual setting as she had at a formal event. Maybe even more so.

While continuing to walk toward the bike path, she glanced over her shoulder to sneak one last glimpse of him. He was dressed in a pair of jeans and a black T-shirt, the soft cotton fabric stretched just snug enough to outline broad shoulders, a hard chest and muscular biceps.

In addition to having a well-toned body, expressive brown eyes and a dimpled smile, he was also an animal lover. Well, maybe he didn't exactly *love* them, but he obviously didn't mind taking someone else's rascally dog for a walk. And that was a good sign, a reason to believe that not all good-looking men were lying, cheating jerks. Right?

Her steps slowed, and she lingered a moment, watching him as he spoke on the phone. That is, until Pepe let out a little bark as if saying "Come on. What are we waiting for?"

"Okay. Let's go." Sofia headed to the condo complex, but her thoughts remained on Beau and what little she'd just learned about him.

He was just as nice and polished as she'd found him before. He was also direct, which she appreciated even though she'd felt a bit awkward when he'd addressed head-on the embarrassment and discomfort they'd both felt that night. *I didn't mean to upset the guy you were with at the Valentine's party.*

She didn't doubt that. She and Beau had only been mingling and chatting, just like the other people at the party, but Beau's presence had definitely set off Patrick.

Beau had been refined and polite. After he turned and walked away, Patrick had glared at her. "What was that all about?"

"Nothing."

"I'm not blind. Or stupid. He was hitting on you. And you liked it."

"Keep your voice down," Sofia said. When he chuffed at the admonition, she added, "Believe it or not, I don't even know his name. We were just making small talk. You didn't have to be so rude."

It had been the second time in their short, two-month relationship that Patrick had made something out of nothing. And when he apologized after the first blowup, he'd seemed remorseful, and she'd given him the benefit of the doubt. But she wasn't up for any repeat performances, especially in a social setting.

As the night unfolded, he continued to remind her that she was out with him and that she ought to stop flirting with other guys. Finally, she'd had enough and insisted on leaving the party early.

Once in the hotel parking lot and standing beside his red Porsche with the driver's door open, Patrick was all smiles again and produced a Tiffany box. "A Valentine's gift," he'd said.

She'd softened a bit, almost forgiving him. Then she read the card that had been addressed to someone else. "Who the hell is Stephanie?"

He'd stammered for a moment, then recovered. "The store made a mistake."

Yeah. Right. "And you implied *I* was cheating?" She'd thrown the box at him and told him she never wanted to see him again.

"Your loss," he said.

As she whipped out her cell phone and called an Uber, he'd peeled out of the parking lot.

All the way home, she'd kicked herself for not

seeing the red flags and ending things sooner. But it was over now. And she'd learned from it. Trust was something to be earned.

She blew out a sigh, and glanced at Pepe, who was happily trotting at her side. "I should have kicked Patrick to the curb when he told me he didn't like dogs. Sheesh. Who wouldn't love a sweet boy like you?"

Pepe wagged his tail as if in total agreement.

"And as luck would have it," she told the sweet dog, "I've crossed paths with Beau again."

She glanced over her shoulder to take one last look at him, but the path had curved and she could no longer see him.

She hadn't noticed his soft Southern drawl at the party, but she'd certainly caught it today. She found it utterly charming. *Do you come here often? About this same time?*

It didn't take a mind reader to know what Beau was getting at. He planned to run into her again— and soon. Her heart spun at the thought.

Wait a second. Thoughts like that were sure to take her down a treacherous rabbit hole that would lead to nowhere good.

Beau was handsome and charming, just like Patrick had been at first. So she'd better be careful. She wasn't about to get carried away by another pretty face. It might be better if she kept her interactions with him contained to the dog park.

Regardless, it was Wednesday evening, and she needed to get home. As usual, her grandmother was making their weekly family dinner. And tonight, she'd promised to make Sofia's favorite meal—*chile verde*, rice, *calabasitas*, homemade flour tortillas and flan for dessert.

Sofia reached down and clipped on Pepe's leash. She didn't mind letting him run free at the park and on the bike trail, but she wasn't taking any chances near the highway.

Minutes later, she arrived at 120 Guadalajara Court, the home she'd purchased for her mom and her paternal grandmother a couple of years ago. It had been the least she could do for the two women who'd loved her unconditionally and had sacrificed so much for her.

After Papa died, Abuelita had moved in to care for Sofia, while Mama worked two jobs to support them.

Pepe let out a little bark and wagged his tail, clearly glad to arrive at his second home. Sofia knocked lightly, then opened the door and stepped into the cozy living room with its polished hardwood floors and white walls adorned with brightly colored Southwestern artwork.

"It's me, Mom." Sofia unhooked Pepe's leash. "We're back."

"Your mama's not here," Abuelita called out. "But she'll be back soon."

Sofia followed her grandmother's voice to the kitchen, relishing the aroma of pork simmering in tomatillos and spice. There she found her grandmother checking a pot on the stove.

"Yum," Sofia said. "Dinner smells good."

"It's almost done, *mija*."

Sofia took a seat at the kitchen table, where the small family of three often gathered for meals, board games and pleasant conversation. "Where'd Mama go?"

Abuelita replaced the lid on the pot, then turned away from the stove. "She went to that little wine shop on the corner. She wanted to buy a bottle of champagne so we could toast your good news."

Sofia broke into a grin. Her news was so much better than good. It was great. Amazing. She'd gotten the call right after she and Pepe arrived at the dog park. As soon as she could catch her breath and contain her excitement, she'd called her mother to tell her that she, Sofia De Leon, the owner and CEO of De Leon Financial Consulting, had been nominated for a Lone Star Best Award. She and the other nominees would be honored at a luncheon in Austin on Friday. There they would receive the instructions on the next round of competition.

She had no idea what to expect, but whatever she had to do, she was going all-in. The publicity

for her investment firm would be priceless. As far
as she was concerned, that award belonged to her,
and she wasn't about to let anyone get in the way.

Chapter Two

Sofia took a seat at the dining room table that was laden with a Mexican feast, while Mama popped the cork on a thirty-dollar bottle of champagne and filled their flutes, the bubbles rising to the top. Then she lifted hers in a toast. "To Sofia, my brilliant, beautiful daughter, the investment whiz who is on everyone's 30-Under-30 list."

"Thank you, Mama." Sofia tapped her glass first against Mama's, then Abuelita's. The resonant sound of crystal-on-crystal filled the small, cozy room. And they each took a sip of bubbly.

"You've worked your tail off to make De Leon Financial Consulting a success," Mama added.

"And now you're finally beginning to reap the rewards and the recognition you deserve."

"*Mija*, I'm so proud of you." Abuelita settled back in her chair at the head of the table, then corrected herself. "I mean, you've always made me proud but especially now that your business is booming. And I love that your focus has been on women."

True. De Leon Financial Consulting was unique. All of Sofia's employees were women, many of them people of color. And so were most of the clients.

Mama let out a soft sigh. "It's too bad I didn't have someone like you to advise me after your papa died."

"I know, Mama." When Sofia was ten, her father died in a work-related accident when he'd been hit by a drunk driver while he was on a highway project. Her mother had received a hefty settlement, but it hadn't lasted long, not when her so-called financial adviser lost the bulk of it. Right then, Mama started learning everything she could about finance and ignited that interest in Sofia. That's why Sofia had double majored in economics and finance—and why she'd eventually left the firm she'd been with and started her own company.

"I couldn't have asked for a better daughter." Mama's eyes filled with happy tears.

Abuelita lifted her champagne glass. "Your father would be so proud to see you now. An MBA and a successful company."

"Thank you, but I couldn't have done it without help from both of you."

They clicked glasses again.

"A master's degree." Abuelita smiled, her eyes glowing misty. "I would have loved to have gone to college when I was young. I used to feel insignificant and ignorant with only a few years of school."

Sofia reached across the table and placed her hand on top of her grandmother's. "You might only have an eighth grade education, but you're one of the brightest and wisest women I know. You don't need a diploma to prove that to me."

The older woman winked. "Thank you, *mija*. Thank you for convincing me otherwise."

"And thank you for trusting me with your hard-earned money. Both of you."

Once Sofia had begun trading and building portfolios, she'd taken over what was left of her mother's small brokerage and savings account, as well as her grandmother's. She made smart trades, and now their investments had grown to the point neither of them had to worry about retirement.

"We better eat while it's still warm," Mama said, as she began to pass around bowls of *chile verde*, rice, beans and *calabasitas*.

Abuelita passed the basket of warm, homemade flour tortillas.

Sofia sat back and watched the women utilize the hospitality skills they'd learned from their own mothers and grandmothers. Meals didn't get any better than this. She looked at them, her heart swelling with love, respect and appreciation— for generations past. Life didn't get any better than this, either.

Her mother scooped a huge spoonful of rice onto Sofia's plate.

"Mama! Not so much. I'll have to let out my pant seams."

Abuelita laughed. "Oh, no. You might balloon up to a size six. *Que lastima.* What a tragedy."

"Speaking of clothes," Mama said, "what are wearing to that luncheon in Austin?"

"I'm not sure. It's a business function. So probably one of the suits I wear to the office."

"Nonsense," Mama said. "You'll need something new. And special. Since I don't have to work tomorrow, I can meet you at your office and we can go shopping for just the right outfit."

"That sounds like fun, but… It's just that…" Sofia shrugged. "Oh, never mind. If it's meant to be, it'll happen."

"What are you talking about?" Abuelita asked.

Sofia waved her off. "You'll think I'm crazy."

"Never." Mama beamed.

Sofia took a deep breath, then slowly let it out. "Remember when I told you about that man I talked to at the Valentine's party? The one that made Patrick angry?"

Abuelita nodded. "He accused you of cheating on him, but it was the other way around. And you found out when he bought gifts for two different women, then mixed up the cards. *El tonto.*"

"Yes, he was a fool. And a jerk. I was going to break up with him anyway. He had a possessive and jealous side. He showed his true colors when he flipped out after seeing me talk to a nice man at the party."

"Aw, *si.*" Abuelita's smile brightened, softening the lines on her face. "*El estrano guapo.*"

Sofia didn't keep too many secrets from her mother or grandmother. "Yes, the handsome stranger." She took a sip of champagne, then chuckled. "Believe it or not, I actually ran into him at the dog park today."

Abuelita clapped her hands gleefully.

"Does *el guapo* have a name?" Mama asked.

"It's Beau. I don't know much about him. Not even his last name. But he was walking a friend's dog, a big, goofy shepherd mix named M.P. He asked if I went to the park very often, and I told him I did—almost daily. So I'm hoping to see him there again."

Abuelita took a tortilla and began to fill it with *chili verde.* "I think you should shop for a new outfit. You two girls deserve a nice afternoon together. Don't worry about Pepe. I'll keep an eye on him. And who knows? I might even take him to the dog park myself."

"Abuelita," Sofia said, "I know that twinkle in your eye. Please. No mischief."

"Me?" Abuelita slapped a hand to her chest, as if offended. "Mischief? When do I ever get up to mischief?"

Whenever the sun rises, Sofia thought. "Promise me?"

Abuelita raised her hand in Girl Scout fashion. "Yes, of course."

Only trouble was, Abuelita had never been a scout.

"It's about that time." Beau snapped the leash on M.P.'s collar. "Come on, boy. Let's go for a walk."

The dog let out an enthusiastic yip, his tail swishing across the coffee table and knocking a travel brochure on the floor.

Once Beau had secured the rambunctious pup, he took him outside and locked the front door. As they started down the walkway, he scanned the post–World War II-style homes that flanked the shady, tree-lined street. He and Draper could have chosen to live in a more exclusive part of town when they moved to Rambling Rose three months ago, but their Fortune cousins had warned them that the locals had a strong resistance to what they referred to as the "Fortune invasion" of the community. Even though it seemed as if the family had finally won over many of the townsfolk, the brothers decided it would be in their best interests to rent a place in a modest neighborhood and show people they weren't pretentious. They'd found a house that was furnished, although they'd only gotten a nine-month lease. The Dobsons were empty nesters who'd taken off on an extended road trip in their RV.

So far, the brothers' plan seemed to be working, because their neighbors were all cordial, if not friendly.

A boy in the backyard of the house to the left of theirs shrieked, "Mom! He did it again! If you don't come out here and make him stop, I'm going to kick his butt."

Beau let out a sigh. Joey and Samantha Billings were nice people. And they seemed like good parents, but they had their hands full with three likable but rambunctious children.

On the other hand, Ginny Sanders, their neighbor to the right, was a quiet schoolteacher. When she wasn't working at Rambling Rose High, she pretty much kept to herself. Sometimes, when Beau mowed the lawn and watered the flower bed near the hedge that grew along the property line, he'd see her painting on her wraparound porch.

They hadn't talked to each other very much, but she seemed nice.

M.P. whined and tugged on the leash impatiently, as if he wanted to dash across the street. When he barked, Beau realized why. Dan Gallagher's Jeep Grand Cherokee had just pulled into the driveway. The dog's master was home, and M.P. was eager to greet him.

When Dan got out of the vehicle, Beau called out, "You're home early. I thought you weren't coming back until tomorrow."

"We had a change of plans." Dan shut the driver's door, then headed toward the street. "My buddy and I cut our fishing trip short. His wife was having some health issues, and he wanted to check on her."

"That's too bad," Beau said.

"I think she'll be okay, but he was worried about her. And I don't blame him. I would have felt the same way."

Other than a nod of acknowledgment, Beau didn't respond. Only six months had passed since Dan lost his wife to cancer. Dan had nursed her until the end, and he was still grieving her loss.

As Dan limped across the street to meet Beau, he said, "Thanks for watching my dog. I hope he wasn't too much trouble for you."

"No problem at all." Well, not really. Beau reached down and stroked M.P.'s head. "We actually had a good time. In fact, I was just going to take him to the dog park and let him run off a little steam."

Dan chuckled. "I don't know what made me think having a young, energetic mutt around would make my house less lonely and quiet. But hell, M.P. would be better off living across the street with the Billings kids. He's got more energy than they do, although just barely."

"Nah, M.P. is a great dog for you. Keeps you young."

"I don't know about that. Sometimes I think I'm falling apart." Dan had been pretty active for a man in his mid-fifties until he'd aggravated an old Army injury.

"How's your knee?" Beau asked.

"Getting better. The doctor doesn't think it'll require surgery, so that's good. But I'm not quite back to fighting weight yet."

Beau probably ought to hand over M.P. to Dan, but he was reluctant to change his plans. How obvious would it be if he showed up at the park without a dog? "Why don't I take M.P. for that walk? That way, you can unpack in peace and quiet. I'll bring him home in an hour or so."

"That'd be great. He'll probably run you into the ground."

Beau laughed. "I don't mind a good workout."

Five minutes later, as the sun sank low in the

Texas sky, Beau reached the park, where several dogs and kids were already playing. M.P. tugged at the leash, eager to join a father and a couple of young boys throwing a ball to a gray, scruffy-looking terrier.

"Settle down, buddy. Let's wait for Sofia and Pepe to show up." Beau glanced at his wristwatch. It was already twenty minutes later today than it had been yesterday when he ran into her. Maybe something came up at work. She said she kept crazy hours.

Unfortunately, he couldn't contain the exuberant pup much longer. He'd no more than unhooked the leash when the goofy mutt dashed off, but not toward the terrier's family. He loped toward an older woman who was walking a fluffy white dog with a red bandana tied around its neck.

"Well, I'll be damned." It was Pepe. And the woman with an olive complexion, her graying hair pulled up in a topknot, must be Sofia's grandmother.

Beau strode toward her, the leash dangling in his hand. "I'm sorry about my dog's lack of manners. We met Pepe here yesterday, and he was eager to play again."

"No need to apologize." She glanced down at M.P., who'd hunched down, tempting Pepe to run off with him. "What a friendly dog you have."

"Thanks. That's true. But he's not mine. He belongs to my neighbor."

She nodded as if she already knew that. "Should we let them loose?"

"Yes. Of course."

As the dogs ran off, she eyed him carefully, looking him up and down. A slow smile tugged at her lips. "You must be Beau."

"That's right." Apparently Sofia had mentioned him to her family. That was a good sign.

"I'm Maria," she said, "Sofia's grandmother."

"I thought so." He offered her a smile. "I see the family resemblance."

"Thank you. She actually looks more like her mother's side of the family, but I'd like to think she has my smile."

"I assume Sofia had to work late."

"Actually, she went shopping with her mother. I'm watching Pepe for her today."

"Good for her," he said. "Sounds like she and her mother are close."

"Yes, they are." Maria's smile faded, and she furrowed her brow. "Aren't you close to your mother?"

"Yes, I guess you could say that. She lives out of state, so I don't see her as often as I used to."

Maria nodded sagely, as if pondering his response, then she added. "Sofia and I are close, too."

"I thought you probably were. Grandparents are special."

"I agree." Again, she eyed him. "Do you have a special grandparent?"

"Yes, my grandmother. I always looked forward to staying with her when I was a kid." Grandma Marjorie was down-to-earth and lived in a modest neighborhood. They'd often go to the bayou, and she taught him and his siblings how to fish and made an amazing crawfish boil. He'd have to plan a visit soon. Phone calls didn't allow for warm hugs.

"Where are you from?" Maria asked.

"New Orleans. I grew up there."

He wouldn't mention that his family lived in the Garden District. Or that his friends often called it a mansion, something that made him feel a little uneasy. The eight-bedroom, ten-thousand-square-foot house might be big by anyone's standards, but it was home to him, the place where he spent all of the memorable holidays, the place where his parents still lived.

"Do you have any siblings?" she asked.

"Yep. Three brothers and three sisters."

"Aw," she said, "you have a large family. That's nice to know."

Was it? What was going on here? Had Sofia sent her grandmother on a fact-finding mission? Oh, what the hell. It wasn't a secret.

"I'm sure your holidays are special," she added. "There's just three of us in our family." She glanced down at the dogs. When she looked up, her brown eyes glistened. "There's a lot to be said for small families, too."

"So it's just Sofia, her mom and you?"

Her eyes misted. "Sofia's papa, my son Ricardo, died when Sofia was a little girl."

"I'm sorry," he said.

"Me, too." She lifted her hand to her forehead, then made the sign of the cross. *"Dios lo tenga en su Gloria."* When her eyes met his, she said, "Do you like Mexican food?"

Who didn't? He nodded. "Yes, I do."

"And home cooking?"

"I love it all, especially if it's homemade but not by me. I tend to either burn my quesadillas or not heat them enough to melt the cheese."

Maria beamed. "Any friend of Sofia's is a friend of mine. So why don't you come for dinner on Saturday?"

Beau didn't know what to say. An invitation like that was a little forward. And so was giving a stranger her address. He hoped she didn't make a habit of it.

As if Maria had read his mind, she said, "You have a kind face. Besides, my granddaughter is a good judge of character, and she thinks you're okay."

A grin tugged at Beau's lips. Sofia had clearly been talking to her family about him.

"So, are you free?" Maria asked. "We can make it a different day, if that would work better for you."

This "surprise" meetup in the park smelled like a setup, but he was eager to see Sofia again—and to learn more about her.

"Actually," he said, "I am free on Saturday. But will that be okay with Sofia? I mean, will she be there? And if so, will she mind that I'm there?"

"No, she'll be fine. Besides, I'm inviting you as my guest. I don't need anyone's approval."

He still thought he ought to run it by Sofia. But when? She wasn't here now. And he had no idea how long he'd be in Austin tomorrow. So, what the hell. "I'll bring a bottle of wine. Just let me know where you live and what time to show up."

She gave him her address, then a wide smile lit her eyes and her softly wrinkled face nearly glowed. "How does four o'clock sound?"

Sofia entered the elegant lobby of the Austin Grand Hotel, her black heels clicking on the Spanish tiled floor. A gurgling water fountain sat in the center of the sprawling space. A sign just to the side of it directed her to the ballroom where the Lone Star Best luncheon would be held.

Her heart pounded in excitement as she turned

down the carpeted corridor and proceeded to the line that had gathered at the registration desk.

She took note of the well-dressed attendees. Each one appeared to be a professional. Were they all nominees? Or guests who'd come in support?

Either way, Mama had been right to insist they go shopping, and the black dress she'd purchased had been the perfect choice.

Her gaze was snagged by a huge flower arrangement on a glass-topped table between two tufted-leather chairs. But it wasn't the colorful flowers that drew a smile, rather the familiar man standing beside them. A man she hadn't expected to see at this particular event. Her heart jumped.

Beau, who wore an expensive dark suit, was talking on his cell phone, his upbeat expression indicating it was a pleasant conversation. Ironic, since he'd been taking a call when she'd last seen him.

Moments later, he pocketed his cell, and when he looked up and caught her eye, he burst into a full-on smile and headed toward her.

She wondered what he was doing here. Then again, the Lone Star Best luncheon attracted a lot of business people.

"What a surprise," he said, as he got into line behind her. "I didn't expect to see you here."

Indeed. What a coincidence. "We seem to run into each other a lot."

She wasn't sure if that was a good thing or not. There was definitely some chemistry between them, but she couldn't help the way her body reacted to him. Besides, she wasn't going to jump into anything. She didn't know anything about him—other than he was gorgeous.

"I see you're registering for the luncheon," he said. "I've already checked in."

So he'd decided to stand beside her while she waited in line? She certainly wouldn't complain about that. Not only did she enjoy talking to him, she liked his alluring scent—a combination of his woodsy aftershave and a manly soap.

Before she could respond, Carla Wynters, the vice president of Rambling Rose Savings and Loan, approached. Sofia as well as De Leon Financial Consulting had several accounts at that bank. They'd become friends last summer after playing on the same team during a softball tournament. They hadn't won, but the proceeds from the games and the dinner/awards ceremony had gone to various local charities.

Carla got in line behind Sofia. With Beau at her side, Carla might think they were a couple. Not that Sofia felt the least bit embarrassed about being seen with such a well-dressed hunk.

"Sofia," the tall, leggy redhead in her midthirties said, "I thought I saw you in the parking lot."

"I'm glad you're here." Sofia offered her a warm smile. "I wasn't sure if I'd know anyone this far from home. Are you nominated for a Lone Star Best Award? Or maybe supporting someone who is?"

"Neither. Actually, my sister has organized the last five events, and I'm her plus-one." Carla offered Beau a smile before returning her attention to Sofia. "I've been meaning to call you and set up another lunch date, but I've been swamped lately."

"Not to worry. So have I." Before Sofia could introduce Beau as her—what? Friend? Acquaintance?—Carla said, "I hope the award goes to someone worthy this year. It seems as though they always award it to the same people. Robinson Tech. Fortune Industries."

"What's wrong with that?" Beau asked.

Carla shrugged. "You know. The ultimate in-crowd. Not always deserving. Inherited wealth and stature. They're born standing on third base and think they hit a triple. But that's life, I suppose. Too bad some of us never had it that easy."

Beau shot a glance at Sofia, and she nodded in agreement.

"That's not fair," he said. "Plenty of people born into a wealthy family work very hard and do a lot of good in the world. Robinson Tech's innovations are legendary. And Fortune Industries led to the Fortune Foundation, which does a lot of good."

"True," Sofia said, "but the Fortune name really does give them advantages. Exposure, for instance. And open doors."

Beau's eyes narrowed, and he stiffened as if taking offense. "Just because a person has money doesn't mean they don't deserve it."

Apparently, the conversation had struck a nerve, which she found more than a little interesting. "You speak like a man who has money."

"And you *don't*?" Beau asked.

Sofia did have money—plenty of it, as Carla was well aware. But Sofia hadn't grown up with it and she'd never had the luxury of taking it for granted. "I get by. But I'm no Fortune."

Beau sobered, and he folded his arms across his broad chest—rather abruptly. "You say the name like it's a dirty word."

At that, Sofia shrugged. "Well, I suppose the Fortunes have their own problems. You have to admit, *mis*fortune follows that family around. Kidnappings, sabotage, drama of all sorts."

"It's as if all that money is a trouble magnet," Carla said. "I'll take my poor relations over that kind of family trouble."

"Would you, now?" Beau glanced at his wristwatch—a Rolex, Sofia noted. Then he looked up and smiled. "If you ladies will excuse me, I'll let you continue your chat. I'm sure we'll see each other around. By the way, I didn't catch your last name, Sofia."

"De Leon," she said. "And yours?"

"It's *Fortune*."

As Beau turned and walked away, warmth flooded Sofia's face as if she'd been in the sun all day. Talk about a major faux pas. She'd just dissed Beau's entire family.

"Well, open mouth and insert foot," Carla said.

"I guess I won't be getting a Fortune account anytime soon." Or a date.

"I'd say that's certainly doubtful."

If Sofia had thought it had been awkward between them at the Valentine's party, things had just gotten ten times worse.

Chapter Three

From the moment Sofia had gotten the phone call telling her she was a nominee for the Lone Star Best Award, she'd been looking forward to this day. But after her awkward blunder in the registration line, the rubber chicken sitting in a pool of gravy on her plate looked scary, and she'd completely lost her appetite. She'd also lost some of her initial enthusiasm.

But hey! She was a competent woman in a man's world. She took things like that in stride. So what if she wished she hadn't commented about the privileged Fortune family. She'd find time to apologize for offending Beau, but in the meantime, she enjoyed the conversation of her tablemates, several of whom asked for her business card.

She took a sip of iced tea, then continued to search the tables, looking for Beau. Aw, there he was. At the opposite side of room, smiling and chatting with the woman seated beside him, a blonde who was leaning toward him, apparently charmed by whatever he said. Yet he glanced across the room and captured her gaze.

A flutter rose up in her chest, and she tamped it down the best she could. Beau Fortune might be tall, dark, handsome and rich, but he wasn't her type. Not by a long shot.

"Ma'am?"

Sofia looked up. One of the servers, a tall, lanky man, had begun to clear the table and was speaking to her. "Yes?"

He pointed at her plate, which she'd hardly touched. "Was something wrong with your meal? Can I get you one of the gluten-free or vegetarian options?"

"No, thank you." She'd found the conversation more palatable than the food.

The microphone at the dais squeaked, and her excitement built again.

"Excuse me." The MC tapped the mic and cleared her throat. "Can I please have your attention?"

A slow hush settled over the ballroom, and the

MC continued, "I'd like to welcome y'all again and thank you for your support. I'm sure you're eagerly awaiting the announcement of this year's nominees. And so, without further ado, I'll do so in alphabetical order." She looked down at the papers on the podium, then began. "De Leon Financial Consulting, represented by the owner, Sofia De Leon. Ms. De Leon, will you please stand?"

Sofia's pride shot through the roof as she got to her feet amid the clapping attendees. She smiled, nodded and then took her seat, thinking the day couldn't get any better. That is, until the MC continued, "Fortune Investments, represented by Beau and Draper Fortune. Unfortunately, Draper wasn't able to attend our luncheon, but his brother Beau is here. Mr. Fortune, would you please stand?"

Sofia's stomach clenched. Thank goodness she hadn't forced down that chicken breast.

Sure, she'd known he was here. She just hadn't expected him to be one of the nominees. And wouldn't you know it? She and Beau represented the same business industry, which meant they'd be in direct competition with each other. That was fine, she told herself. She could handle that. And no matter how awkward things were between them, she was determined to take home the Lone Star Best Award and display it in the lobby of her firm.

As the next several nominees were announced,

she found herself looking for Beau again. She hadn't meant to insult him or his family, even though what she'd said was true. She hated to see another Fortune company snag yet another award. After the luncheon, she would find him and tell him she was sorry, although she doubted a simple apology would set things right between them. He seemed to be pretty thin-skinned. Not that it mattered, she supposed. Ever since she ended things with Patrick, she'd decided to focus on her work, where she felt validated and could see tangible results of her efforts, instead of dating guys who turned out to be players. Or, in Beau's case, guys with whom she'd have to walk on eggshells.

"Ma'am," the server said, interrupting her thoughts again. "Should I leave the dessert?"

Sofia glanced at the decadent chocolate mousse torte. It would be a shame to send it back to the kitchen. "Yes, please. I can always find room for chocolate."

As the server continued to clear the table, Sofia again caught sight of Beau. The thirtyish blonde leaned toward him, cupped her hand over her mouth as if whispering something, and they both laughed.

That fluttery butterfly feeling returned, building like the flapping wings of a southbound flock of geese.

Dammit, Sofia. You don't have a blasted thing

to be jealous about. Let it go. One of the Fortunes, no matter how handsome and charming, was the last man in the world she needed to have feelings for. She snatched her fork and cut into the torte.

The microphone at the dais squeaked. "Excuse me." The MC tapped the mic and cleared her throat. "I know y'all are busy congratulating the nominees, but I'd like to explain the rules of the first of two rounds of the competition."

Sofia couldn't wait to hear the rules. After all, she had no doubt whom she'd be vying against. She lifted her fork and took a bite of the torte. *Umm.* It was delicious. And much sweeter than she'd expected.

"The Lone Star Best committee has carefully drawn up teams," the MC said.

Teams? Sofia set down her fork. How was that going to work? Should she be taking notes?

"Each team has been assigned to either a social or charity project in their various communities. Their work will be judged, and they'll earn points. The two teams with the most points will move on to the final round."

An older man sitting next to Sofia chuckled. "I'm glad I'm not in the running this year."

Why? Had the rules changed? It seemed like it, but so what? It didn't really matter anyway. Sofia was going all-in and intended to win—no matter what her assignment.

"If each of the nominees will come to the dais," the MC said, "we'll give you the name of your teammate and your project."

The nominees began rising and moving to the front of the room, although Beau didn't appear to be in any hurry. He probably figured that with his name and connections, he'd be a shoo-in. But Sofia had no intention of making it easy for him.

When she reached the dais, a balding gentleman stationed there looked at the name tag she wore, then handed her a white envelope. "Ah, Ms. De Leon. Here you go. You'll find contact information inside the envelope."

Sofia thanked him. As she turned away, she glanced at the printing on the front of the envelope and damn near choked when she spotted the two familiar names. Sofia De Leon and Beau Fortune.

Oh, no. That wasn't going to work. She turned back around. "Excuse me, sir. There must be some mistake. How can two direct competitors be on the same team?"

"It's not a mistake," he said. "You'll see that your assignment is at Rambling Rose High School. And since you and Mr. Fortune both live and work in the area, it makes perfect sense for you to join forces."

Perfect sense to whom? Certainly not to Sofia. "I really don't think Mr. Fortune and I can work together."

"I'm sure you'll do just fine," the man said. "It is, after all, a very good cause."

She let out a sigh of frustration, then turned away. Before she could take a step, she spotted Beau two feet to her right. A frown and a furrowed brow indicated that he'd just heard her try to get out of collaborating with him.

Great. Not only were they off to a very bad start because of her big mouth, it looked as if they were stuck with each other. But she made the first move and closed the small gap between them. "I'm sorry if I offended you."

"Just now? Or earlier?"

"Both. When I saw who I was supposed to work with, I thought it might be difficult."

"For you? Or for me?"

"Both of us. We have history."

"Barely speaking to each other at a party and meeting in a dog park is hardly history. Be honest, Sofia. You seemed to like me until you found out who my family is."

True. But she was learning more about who he was, and now she had doubts about him. But she opted to keep her mouth shut for fear she'd stick her foot in it again.

"Believe it or not," he said, "I'm not surprised. I've gotten used to the fact that people often make assumptions about me based solely on my last name. That's why my brother and I have tried to keep a low profile in the community."

Yeah, right. A man who was that blasted gorgeous and so well-dressed couldn't keep a low profile if he tried. But she'd be damned if she'd respond to whatever game he was playing. The stakes were too high.

"That said," Beau added, "I'm not sure how the point system will come into play, but for starters, we're going to have to cooperate. I hope you can put your animosity and distrust of me and my family aside so we do right by the people in our community."

"I don't have much choice."

"Of course you do. You can drop out of the competition if this seems too hard for you."

What an arrogant jerk. "Not on your life, buddy." She mustered a smile and reached out her hand. "How about a truce? At least, temporarily."

His dark brow arched. "Only temporarily?"

"Until our project is complete."

He took her hand, his fingers wrapping around hers in a firm but gentle grip that radiated heat all the way to her shoulder. "Then it's back to disliking me and my family?"

"I don't dislike your family. Or you. I've never met them, and as you said, I hardly even know you."

"Good." He released her hand. "Then, we might even become friends."

"I'm not so sure about that." His privilege, the fact that she'd had to struggle and bust her butt for everything she had and he'd stepped right into his made it damn near impossible that anything serious—or lasting—would form between them.

"What makes you so doubtful?" he asked.

She offered him a playful grin and lifted the unsealed white envelope as if it were a flag of truce—when, in reality, it was anything but. "I'll do my best to work with you on this project and knock it out of the park. But I intend to win the Lone Star Best Award, Mr. Fortune, and I plan to smoke you to the finish line. So bring on your A game. You're going to need it."

Then she turned on her heel and headed out of the ballroom, fighting the urge to look over her shoulder to see if he was watching.

Beau had the heart of a competitor and couldn't help picking up the gauntlet Sofia had thrown down. He also had the heart and soul of a healthy male, which was why he watched her stride out of the ballroom, his gaze locked on the sway of her hips and the hem of her black dress as it swished against her shapely legs.

Damn, the woman was as sexy as hell, especially when she was both flustered and angry.

He had to admit he'd been offended by her off-hand remark about the Fortunes. But like he'd told her, he wasn't prone to being overly sensitive and easily insulted. At least, not for very long.

Besides, her attitude about his family hadn't taken him by surprise. There was still a sizable contingent of Rambling Rose residents who felt the same way she and her friend did. Hell, even back in New Orleans when he was in elementary school, he'd been painfully aware of the reaction people had to his last name alone. He'd always wondered if things might have been different if his mother had won the arguments over a private school versus public. But his father, who could have well afforded to pay for all seven of his children to attend an elite and prestigious academy, had insisted that his children would be more grounded in the real world if they went to public school.

Still, it had bothered Beau when his friends had visited his house in the Garden District and referred to it as a mansion, then oohed and aahed over his family's belongings. Or, when he'd aced a final exam or excelled in sports, someone always seemed to tell him they'd do well, too, if they could afford fancy tutors or private coaches. Hell, how about having self-discipline and putting in a lot of hard work?

And now here he was, trying to stay grounded while living in Texas.

On his way out of the ballroom, he took a look

at the white envelope he'd been given. He suspected it was identical to the one Sofia had.

Once he'd gotten into his car, he opened it and skimmed the contents. Now, that was interesting. They'd be creating and overseeing a personal finance project at Rambling Rose High School—another assignment his brother Draper would probably find a reason to skip out on. But what the hell. Beau rather liked the idea of working with Sofia on his own, without having his brother around.

Interestingly enough, this was going to take some prep time, too. Getting together over coffee. Maybe a lunch meeting or two to work out the perfect game plan that would appeal to teenagers and stretch their knowledge of the financial world. He wondered how Sofia was going to feel about that.

He supposed he'd find out tomorrow at four o'clock, when he arrived at her grandmother's house for dinner.

After all, he'd already told Maria he was coming. And if she was anything like his own grandma, she'd already started cooking and preparing to host a guest.

Something told him Sofia would get her panties in a wad... A smile stretched across his face. They'd be pretty ones. Silky. Skimpy...

Dammit, man. This isn't the time to think about

her that way. They were supposed to work together, not play together. It was also for a good cause. Besides, they were competitors in business and for a Lone Star Best Award. And with her preconceived notion about him and his family, that's all they'd ever be.

Rather than head back to the office to tie up any loose ends, Sofia trusted her executive assistant to do that for her. Instead, she left the hotel in Austin and drove straight to her mother's condo, ready to vent to the two women she loved most in the world. And a bottle of wine would be involved.

She knocked lightly at the door, then let herself inside. Pepe greeted her with a yip and a wagging tail. She stooped to give him a hug and an ear scratch. "Did you miss me?"

"Oh, good," Mama said. "It's you."

Sofia straightened, but her smile faded when she caught the scent of lemon oil and spotted Mama with a roll of paper towels in one hand and a plastic carrier filled with cleaning supplies in the other. She placed both near a step stool that had been put in front of the living room window.

"What are you doing?" Sofia asked. "Doesn't the housekeeper come on Monday?"

"Yes." Mama chuckled. "But it's time for a little spring cleaning. And after that last rain, I thought

I'd wash the windows. Besides, your abuelita has invited a guest for dinner tomorrow."

Sofia was glad her mom and grandmother were making friends in the neighborhood. A couple of weeks ago, they'd invited Dottie, who lived on Calle Veracruz, for lunch. But they hadn't gone to this much trouble.

"How was the luncheon?" Mama asked.

"It was okay. I'll tell you all about it—once I open a bottle of wine."

"Mija?" Abuelita called from the kitchen. "Is that you?"

"Yes, it's me."

"Good. You're just in time to help me take the good china from the hutch. I want to wash it."

"Wow." Sofia laughed. "Her guest must be someone special."

"She thinks so." Mama turned and blessed her with a smile. "She says it's a secret. She won't even tell me."

"Hmm. I wonder who it could be. Don't tell me she invited the older man who just moved in across the street. I think she has a little crush on him."

"Maybe so. You know what a flirt she is. Who can resist her when she lays on the charm?"

Sofia placed her purse on the overstuffed chair near the hearth. "I'll get those dishes for her. But let me know when you can take a break."

Mama frowned and lifted one hand. "Window

washing?" She lifted the other hand, as if balancing options on a scale. "A bottle of my favorite merlot?" Then she clapped them together and laughed. "*Mija*, the cleaning can wait. Let's go open that wine."

Several minutes later, Sofia pulled the cork out of the bottle of merlot. Then she filled three glasses and took a seat at the table.

"Did things go that badly?" Mama asked.

"No, I wouldn't say that. The nominees all felt honored. But…" Sofia sucked in a deep breath, then slowly blew it out. "It's just that I said something to someone I wish I hadn't. Not that it wasn't exactly how I felt, but I insulted him. And I hadn't meant to."

"That doesn't sound like you." Mama lifted her glass and took a sip. "Go on. What happened?"

Sofia told them about seeing Beau at the luncheon and learning that his last name was Fortune. But, regrettably, not until after she'd made some disparaging comments about his family.

"And you had no idea who his family is before today?" Abuelita clicked her tongue. "The Fortunes are all very rich. And influential."

"Yes, I know. They were all born into money. The whole privileged lot of them. And then there's the fact that a few of their companies have already won a Lone Star Best Award."

"You're afraid you won't be treated fairly?" Mama asked.

"Yes. No. Maybe." Sofia lifted her glass, her fingers trembling slightly, although she doubted anyone noticed. "It's just that I've worked my fanny off to be where I am today, and I want to snag that award for De Leon Financial Consulting. At any cost."

Mama beamed. "That's my girl. A fighter. And a winner."

"So what seems to be the problem?" Abuelita asked.

Sofia explained the first round of the competition. "And guess who I was teamed up with for a project at the high school? Beau Fortune."

"Oh, wow," Mama said. "Awkward."

Sofia chuffed. "No kidding."

Abuelita cleared her throat and mumbled something incoherent. Sofia turned to her grandmother. "What's that?"

Her grandmother looked first to the left, then shifted her eyes to the right. But instead of answering, she picked up her wineglass and took a drink.

"Mama Maria," Sofia's mother said, "did I hear you correctly? Did you say 'not as awkward as tomorrow'?"

Still no response. Apparently, she'd clammed up. "Okay," Sofia said. "Abuelita, you'd better spill."

The sweet older woman set down her glass and

turned to Sofia, her big brown eyes glimmering
and the hint of a grin tugging at her lips. She gave
a little shrug. "Guess who's coming to dinner?"

Chapter Four

Sofia couldn't believe her grandmother had invited the enemy to dinner. Okay, so Beau Fortune wasn't actually her enemy. He was, however, her competitor in the business world as well as in the race for the Lone Star Best, an award they were each determined to win. And that made socializing out of the question, but here she was at Mama's house, waiting for Beau's arrival. Damn.

She could have easily found something to keep her busy on a lovely Saturday afternoon, something that would give her a good excuse to skip out on dinner. But she didn't dare leave Abuelita and Beau unsupervised. Who knew how that conversation might unfold? Or what insights Beau might nudge out of the two older women who were scurrying around the condo like they were expecting royalty.

Both Mama and Abuelita enjoyed having company, so Sofia wasn't entirely surprised by their hospitality efforts. She just hoped the red-carpet treatment didn't have anything to do with Beau's last name.

She glanced at the antique clock on the mantel. It had been a gift to Abuelita's parents on their wedding day. Sofia couldn't remember when it hadn't held a special place of honor in her grandmother's home—and now here it was in the condo she shared with Mama.

As it neared four o'clock, the pendulum seemed to swing faster and faster with each tick-tock.

Sofia rolled her eyes. Then she returned to the dining room, where Abuelita was carrying a fresh bouquet of daffodils to the table set for four. Her grandmother had used the china, crystal and silverware, new heirlooms that hadn't been in the De Leon family very long. "A housewarming gift," Sofia had explained to her mom when she'd given them to her.

Other than holidays, Mama rarely used them. So why now? Why the fuss?

"Abuelita," Sofia said, "we don't usually eat

dinner before five or five thirty. So why on earth did you tell Beau to come at four?"

"I thought it would be nice to get to know him better, *mija*. But that was before I knew you disliked him and his family."

"*Dislike* isn't the right word," Sofia said.

Abuelita placed the flowers in the center of the table then straightened. "Then, what is the right word?"

"Well, he's my competitor for one thing—in business and for the Lone Star Best Award."

"Hmm." Abuelita scrunched her nose. "You have to admit, your Mr. Fortune is *muy guapo y simpatico*."

Sofia folded her arms across her chest. "Does being handsome and charming mean that a man is trustworthy or loyal? You do realize that it's also the mark of a con man."

"Yes, that's possible, I suppose. It's just that he reminded me of your grandfather. My Carlos was handsome and charming, too." The seventy-five-year-old widow's eyes grew a little too misty for Sofia's comfort. "I'm sorry I invited him, *mija*. I thought it would be a nice surprise for you, and I was wrong. But he's my guest, so I hope you'll be nice to him, even if you don't really like him. After all, he was doing his neighbor a favor by walking his dog. Isn't that a good sign of his character?"

Abuelita's fondness for Beau was certainly obvious. It was also a bit irritating. "You've sure gone all out for him. I'm surprised you didn't hire mariachis and rent a margarita fountain."

Abuelita clapped her hands. "Now, why didn't I think of that? I love a fiesta."

"So do I, but something tells me this evening is going to be anything but festive."

Mama entered the room carrying a tray laden with a basket of homemade tortilla chips and bowls of salsa *fresca* and guacamole. "Maria, where do you want me to put this?"

"In the living room, on the coffee table. Then tell Alexa to play some mariachi music."

"Good idea," Mama called out.

Sofia was about to object when Pepe began to bark like crazy, the music started to play and the doorbell rang.

After the luncheon in Austin, Beau had considered telling Sofia's grandmother that something unexpected had come up and he wouldn't be able to have dinner at her house on Saturday. But since he only had her address, he would've had to just show up and tell her in person.

The Lone Star Best folks had included Sofia's contact information in his instruction packet, so a simple phone call to her would have worked, but he'd decided to leave her out of the loop and show up at the scheduled time. So here he was, holding a bottle of his favorite Mendoza Winery merlot and standing on Maria's front stoop, next to a clay pot filled with bright red geraniums.

Beau had no more than rung the bell when the playful Pepe he knew morphed into watchdog mode, announcing his arrival with a barrage of barks.

"*Callate*, Pepe," a female voice called out. "Shush. Quiet down."

When the door opened, Beau was greeted by the sounds of a mariachi band and a fifty-something brunette who wore her hair in a pixie cut. She was bent in an effort to get a grip on Pepe's collar, holding him from dashing after the intruder.

The moment Pepe recognized Beau, he quieted but he wiggled and wagged his tail as if he expected to see M.P. jump out from behind the geraniums and barge into the house for a doggy play date.

The woman released Pepe and straightened. Her brown eyes lit up when she smiled. "I'm Camila De Leon, Sofia's mother."

No surprise there.

"You must be Mr. Fortune," she added.

"Please. Call me Beau."

She stepped aside to let him into the living room. After she shut the door, he handed her the bottle of merlot.

"Thank you. But you didn't need to bring anything."

"I'm a Southern boy. My mom and grandma taught me to never show up empty-handed. I hope you like wine."

"Yes, we all do. So thank you. I'll be happy to uncork this and serve it, but there are other options. Maria has whipped up her homemade sangria. And she makes the best margaritas in Texas."

"Both sound amazing," he said. "So don't bother opening the wine. Save it for another time."

Approaching footsteps sounded upon the Spanish-tile floor. Beau looked up to see Sofia enter the room. Her brown eyes gleamed, and her long, dark hair hung loose about her shoulders. The top two buttons of her red blouse were tastefully undone, revealing a shapely neck that practically begged to be nuzzled, a smooth swatch of tanned skin adorned with a single diamond on a delicate silver chain. Black jeans hugged her hips, and he couldn't help letting his eyes trail down her gorgeous legs to a pair of sandals that showcased her red-painted toenails.

Damn, she looked good. From the top to the bottom and back up again. Of course, she'd look even better if she wore a smile.

"Your, uh…" Words failed him for a beat, which was unusual, but he quickly recovered. "Your grandmother invited me to dinner."

"Yes, I know." And she was clearly not happy to see him here.

"I assume you're joining us." When she nodded, he asked, "Do you mind talking business for a few minutes?"

"Not at all. We may as well put our time here to good use."

As opposed to what? Their time together being a complete waste? He wasn't sure how to take her comment, but he shook it off and got down to brass tacks. "I've been looking over the Lone Star Best instructions and had a few ideas I'd like to bounce off you."

"I've given them some thought, too."

"That's good," Camila said, reminding them both that she'd been listening to the awkward greeting. "I know how important your project is to both of you. Why don't you have a seat and chat while I put this wine in the kitchen. Can I bring you a margarita or a glass of sangria, Mister—I mean, Beau?"

"I've always been partial to margaritas," he said. "Thank you, ma'am."

Camila's warm gaze traveled to Sofia. *"Mija?"*

Finally, at the Spanish term of endearment, a slow smile spread across Sofia's face. Her stance, as well as her tone, softened. "I'll have the sangria. *Gracias, Mama.*"

Sofia pointed to a comfy-looking sofa that sat

against the window. Waning afternoon sunlight shined through the shutter and onto the backrest. "Have a seat."

Beau did as Sofia suggested, then watched her sit in an overstuffed chair upholstered in a brightly colored Southwestern print. Pepe curled up at her feet.

"What are you thinking?" she asked.

"You look really nice."

She blinked. "Thanks, but let's focus on the project. So what are your thoughts?"

That she was a lovely woman—from head to toe. And that he'd lose his edge when it came to business if he wasn't careful. But she was clearly talking about their project at the high school.

"Have you ever played *The Game of Life*?" he asked. "It's a board game that's been around for years."

She nodded. "Yes, I'm familiar with it."

"What if we assigned the students mock professions, paycheck stubs and a mortgage payment? We could teach them about balancing a checkbook, budgeting and saving for a rainy day. Maybe we could even show them how to file a tax return."

"We should definitely talk about investing," she said.

"Yes, of course. But first we could also talk to them about taxes, not to mention taking out student loans."

She slowly nodded. "I see where you're going with this. And I like it. But keep in mind that not every student will be going to college. Some will go to trade school."

"True. Or join the military. Or go straight to work."

Her brow furrowed, and she seemed to drift off for a moment, then she gazed at him. "In those mock scenarios, maybe we should hit them with a crisis of some kind—an unexpected death of a spouse or a disability or a fire that damages the house. How will they live if they don't have a savings account or some kind of financial planning?"

"Good idea. And they should also know how to deal with positive windfalls. Like a major promotion and salary increase, even a lottery win. Or maybe a big recording contract? Or acting in a hit TV show."

"Oh, I like that. They can pull cards at random, just like in real life. They'll get stuck with the good and the bad." She paused, then arched a brow. "Most will have been born with a plastic spoon instead of a silver one."

And there it was. The dig. But he'd send it right back to her, putting his own spin on it. "Yes. And either way, they need to be smart enough to use whatever they were dealt to create the best life they can. And don't forget. We're all doing life the best we can." He paused for a beat as another thought sprang up. "Let's also add a community service element, so we can encourage them to consider how they can use their resources to help those who aren't as fortunate. Just like my parents taught me."

He waited for a skeptical remark or expression. Instead, she nodded. "I like that."

Sofia's mother returned to the living room with a large goblet of sangria and a salt-rimmed glass filled with a slushy margarita. "Here you go," she said, as she passed them out.

"Thank you." Beau studied the glass for a moment. The afternoon sunlight pouring through the window danced on the salt crystals, making them glisten. "This sure looks good."

"Wait until you taste it. You won't be disappointed." Camila offered him a smile, then brightened. "Would you like me to bring you a pad and a pen? That way, you can make notes."

"Thank you, Mama. I must admit that we seem to have come up with some good ideas. I'm actually looking forward to meeting those kids and helping them make good financial decisions."

"And maybe good life decisions, too," Beau added.

Sofia gave him a thumbs-up and sipped her drink.

As Maria hurried from the room, Beau turned to Sofia. "See? With us working together, we came up with a game plan. That's called teamwork."

"Maybe that's the point of our first assignment," she said.

Distracted for a second by the tip of her tongue making a quick lick across her lips, he cleared his throat. "Yes. The awards committee knows we're leaders in our industry. Now they want to see how we work as a team."

"You're probably right. And I..." She studied the goblet as if trying to decide whether it was half full or half empty. Then she set down her drink, looked at him and sighed. "I'm sorry, Beau. We got off on the wrong foot at the luncheon—mostly because of my comments about your family and others who've had life easier than the rest of us. If you won't hold that against me, I think we can do a great job on the high school project."

"I've never been one to hold a grudge. So, yes. I'll forgive you. Let's show the other nominees how financial competitors can join forces and knock it out of the park. We can worry about round two later."

There was no denying that he was right. Sofia knew working as a team and creating a top-notch program for those kids was the only way either of them could take the lead in round two.

"Listen, Beau. I want to win the Lone Star Best as badly as you do. Maybe even more. So yes, I can put aside our differences and work together."

"All right." He lifted his margarita and pointed it toward her drink, silently suggesting that they toast their joint venture.

She tapped her goblet against his glass, indicating her agreement. "Then, let's do it. And do it big."

After discussing days and times they'd both be available, they settled on Tuesday and Thursday afternoons, but acknowledged that they'd have to alter their schedules if the school had a conflict.

"I'll contact the principal and see what she has to say. I'll keep you posted." Sofia took a sip of the sangria. Yum. Abuelita made the best drinks.

Mama entered the living room, her cheeks flushed, her eyes bright. "Dinner's ready."

Sofia got to her feet and glanced at Beau. "Shall we?"

"Sounds good to me." He stood and followed her into the dining room.

In spite of her initial uneasiness, dinner turned out to be a pleasant experience. Abuelita had outdone herself in creating a Mexican feast. And even though the two older women's curiosity bordered on an inquisition at times, everyone seemed to have an enjoyable evening.

Beau and Sofia continued to talk about the project at Rambling Rose High—until Abuelita dropped a metal serving spoon onto the tile floor.

"Here," Beau said. "Let me get that for you."

As he reached to pick it up off the floor, the older women launched into a whispered conversation in Spanish.

He's such a gentleman, Mama said.

Abuelita responded, *Didn't Sofia's old boyfriend have problems getting along with his parents? This one has a lot of respect for his mother and grandmother.*

Sofia rolled her eyes, but she let their chatter go. That is, until Mama said, *I like him.*

Me, too. Abuelita broke into a smile that could compete with a successful matchmaker working for an online dating service.

"Please stop," Sofia told the well-meaning women in English. "It's rude to speak in Spanish when we have a guest." She turned to Beau. "I'm sorry."

"No problem," Beau said.

When Abuelita told Mama—in Spanish yet again!—that she thought Sofia and Beau made a handsome couple, Sofia's cheeks flamed. She'd had enough. Dammit, the man was going to think the De Leons had been born in a barn and had never learned any social skills or manners.

"It's time for Pepe's evening walk," Sofia said. "Mama, why don't you and Abuelita take him tonight while I clean up the kitchen?"

"And I'll help her," Beau said.

The women nearly fell over themselves getting

Pepe's leash, giggling like a couple of schoolgirls. As they led the happy dog into the living room, Abuelita muttered something about leaving the two lovebirds alone. For once this evening, Sofia was glad they were speaking Spanish.

Five minutes later, while Beau and Sofia were washing and drying the last of the dishes, their conversation turned once again to the high school project.

"I worked as a teacher's assistant when I was in graduate school. The professor had some serious health issues at times, and I'd have to give the lecture." Sofia reached for the red bowl that once held the rice. "So I have some experience teaching in an academic setting. But those students weren't teenagers."

"I know what you mean," Beau said, as he dried the last plate and stacked it on the counter with the other three. "I guess we'll just have to remember what it was like when we were that age."

"I'll certainly try." But Sofia doubted that it would be easy. She'd been so focused on getting accepted to a good college and receiving a scholarship that she'd skipped a lot of the usual social activities—like going to the prom, playing sports and attending games. And she'd been too busy for the usual teenage drama and angst. Except for once—in college, when the dorm roommate she'd considered the sister she'd never had went behind her back and made a play for the guy Sofia had been dating.

Not that Sofia and James had made a serious romantic commitment, but she cared about him, so they might have. Eventually. And it still hurt to think the two people she'd trusted completely had betrayed her.

After calling home and venting to her mother, she'd taken Mama's advice about men, believing there'd be plenty of time to date later, after she got a degree. But then she focused on her career, so dating had never been that high on her priority list. Maybe, if she'd had more experience when it came to romance, she would have seen through Patrick sooner.

She'd learned a valuable lesson, though. Trust had to be earned. And self-reliance was an absolute necessity.

"What was your favorite subject in high school?" Beau asked.

"Math, I suppose. I also liked history." She reached for the bowl he'd just dried so she could put it back into the cupboard. "How about you?"

"Español."

Spanish? The bowl slipped from Sofia's hands, landed on the ceramic tile floor and shattered into pieces along with her pride. "Are you kidding me? You knew what my mother and grandmother were saying to each other? Why didn't you tell me?"

"I just did." He tossed her a boyish grin. "But why ruin their fun? I don't always know what other people have on their minds."

"Too bad you can't read my mind right now."

He grinned. "Oh, I think I can. In both languages."

"Smart aleck." Sofia pulled out the trash can, as well as a broom and dustpan. "You could have said something to them and nipped their silly chatter in the bud."

"I thought it was funny." Beau stooped to help her pick up the big pieces of broken glass, then he took the broom from her. "I'll sweep up the rest of it."

Sofia might have insisted upon doing it herself, but she took a step back and let him clean up instead. After all, she wouldn't have dropped the bowl if he hadn't been so tight-lipped and sneaky.

"Most people have no idea that I'm bilingual," Beau said. "I even know a lot of the slang terms."

The swear words, too, she suspected. "Where did you pick that up?"

"When I was a senior, I was chosen to take part in a foreign exchange student program. I polished my conversational skills in Guadalajara. And it wasn't all study time. I was able to socialize and make friends."

"Chosen, huh?" She slung the kitchen towel

over her shoulder. This guy got everything handed to him.

His eyes narrowed, and in a low tone, he said, "It had nothing to do with my last name, if that's what you're implying."

Yeah, right. "We're on equal ground now, and all that matters is that we work together and get through to the next round of the Lone Star Best."

"I couldn't agree more."

And then she was going to smoke him.

In the meantime, she'd learned a valuable lesson when it came to working with or competing with Beau Fortune. If he ever had the inside track, he'd keep it close to the vest.

And it would be in Sofia's best interest to do the same.

Chapter Five

At a quarter to three on Tuesday afternoon Beau waited in front of the Rambling Rose High School library for Sofia. They'd agreed to meet here since they'd been assigned to one of two special classrooms inside the building.

He'd arrived early, hoping to beat her here. She must have had the same idea because he'd hardly scanned the lawn in front of the Spanish Mission–style school, complete with a bell tower, when he spotted her approaching. She held a large red box against her right hip and gripped the handle of a black leather briefcase in her left hand.

He strode toward her, unable to help scanning

the length of her. She'd swept up her hair in a stylish topknot befitting a prim and proper librarian. She'd also dressed for the occasion in a black business suit. On the other hand, he'd chosen a more casual outfit—khaki slacks and a black polo shirt.

She looked him up and down. "Just step off the golf course?"

"Nope. You just come from a funeral?"

When she rolled her pretty brown eyes, he chuckled. "I must admit, it doesn't matter what you have on, you wear sexy well."

"Spoken as a real player—and I'm not talking about golf."

He'd never been a player. That was more Draper's M.O. Still, he gave her a wink, then reached for the box. "Here. Let me take that for you."

"Thanks."

He peered into the box, which was full. "What have you got in here?"

"For one thing, those cards we talked about. My executive assistant picked them up at the printer this morning."

"We could have worked on those together," he said.

"I know. But I wanted to make sure they were done just right."

"Thanks, although I would have liked to have had more input."

"I thought we'd agreed and that I wouldn't need your approval. We can both share the credit."

"Or take the blame."

She rolled her eyes. "Don't worry about that. It's going to work perfectly."

Just the way she wanted it to. She was a control freak, it seemed. And a pretty one at that. Still, he ought to be annoyed with her, and he was. But he had to admit, he sort of admired her spunk, too.

As they strode toward the library entrance, the soft, floral scent of her perfume swirled around him, casting some kind of mesmerizing spell on him. He did his best to tamp down the attraction he'd felt since the first moment he saw her at the dance, but he wasn't having much luck.

"Are you ready to face the masses?" she asked.

"As ready as I'll ever be." He shifted the box to one arm, then opened the door for her.

Once inside, they were greeted by a forty-something brunette wearing a big teeth-whitening-enhanced smile.

"You must be Mr. Fortune and Ms. De Leon. I'm Fiona Prather, the school librarian. Let me show you to your classroom."

They followed her past a bulletin board displaying a variety of old photographs depicting life in nineteenth-century Rambling Rose. Beau would have liked to study the photos a bit more carefully, but they both arrived early for a reason—to get set up for their first presentation.

"We have twenty-two seniors attending your class," Fiona said. "And six juniors. I'm sure they're eager to hear what you have to say."

Not if they were anything like some of the kids he'd known at his high school. Seniors could be a tough crowd. They might be on the verge of adulthood, but they didn't always realize they weren't as smart as they'd be in a few years.

"Your program sounds fascinating," Fiona added. "If I didn't have to man the reference desk this afternoon, I'd ask you if I could sit in on it. My grandfather passed away recently and left me a small inheritance, and I'm not sure what to do with it. I could use a little financial guidance. I have a friend who blew through a similar amount of money. It was gone before she knew it, and all she had to show for it was a few pairs of shoes, if you know what I mean."

"I do know what you mean." Sofia reached into her pocket and handed her a business card. "Give me a call. I'd be happy to talk to you and offer some suggestions."

"Great. I will."

Always on the ready, huh? Sofia sure pounced on the opportunity to snag a new client. But that was okay. He didn't usually work with small investors, although he would have passed her on to an associate.

Fiona opened the door to a classroom. "Make yourselves at home. There's a coffeepot in my office. If you'd like a cup, let me know. I'll bring it to you."

"I'm fine." Sofia glanced at Beau. "How about you?"

"Maybe after class."

Fiona glanced at the clock on the wall. "The bell will ring at 3:05. Then the kids will start filing into the room." She turned to go, then stopped. "By the way, I heard a couple of the boys talking. They read the program description, but they seem a little unsure of what to expect."

Truth be told, Beau was a little unsure, too. "We've tried to make this class both fun and informative, so I think they'll actually enjoy it."

"I'm sure they will," Fiona said. "There's something else you might want to keep in mind. Rambling Rose High School reflects the two societies that exist in town. There are the usual haves and the have-nots. Most of the haves come from the new influx of people who've moved to town. And those of more modest means are the ones who've been here for years."

"I'm not surprised," Sofia said. "I think we've got that covered. Beau and I represent those same groups."

He clamped his mouth shut. He wasn't up for another verbal sparring match. Not in front of the school librarian. Besides, the students would be arriving soon, and he wanted to make a good first impression.

But damn. Was she going for another dig because he was new in town and came from a wealthy family? It sure seemed that way. But he wasn't about to apologize for the way he was brought up—or for running a company that catered to the rich and famous. And while Beau didn't usually mingle with people who were in the middle or working class, other than his current neighbors and his former high school classmates and teammates, it's not like he was out of touch.

And as for Sofia, she might have grown up poor, but look at her now. She was clearly on the fast track to wealth and success.

Before he knew it, Sofia had emptied her red box and spread the cards and worksheets on the teacher's desk.

"Boy," he said. "You sure are organized."

She looked up. "Yes, I am. I know this is supposed to be teamwork, but I've never worked with you before. I wasn't sure what to expect, so I took the ball and ran with it."

In a way, he'd been glad she had. He'd had a busy week at the office. But he'd always been a team player—and he never dropped the ball. "Just don't forget whose idea it was."

She tensed and slapped her hands on her hips. "I'm well aware of that. But are you kidding me? We brainstormed the hell out of your initial idea."

"Okay, good point. And I'll admit you took it to the next level."

Her lips parted, but before she could respond, the bell rang, and the school seemed to come alive with the sounds of doors opening and closing amid a cacophony of teenage chatter.

"Ready or not," Sofia said, "here they come."

As the kids began to fill the classroom and take their seats, Beau had a momentary flash of his own high school days and being forced to take a course he hadn't signed up for. When a tall, lanky boy came in wearing a shirt with a *Breakfast Club* logo, Beau bit back a grin. He loved that movie. It was a classic.

He couldn't help wondering if that's how the kid felt this morning while getting dressed, like he was being punished and was being sent to some kind of detention.

A couple of girls walked in, one of whom had colored her platinum-blond hair with streaks of pink. She'd dressed colorfully in a short ruffled skirt and black fishnet stockings and lace gloves. She reminded him of a young Cyndi Lauper.

The bell rang a second time, the voices quieted and they all took a seat.

"Good afternoon," Beau said. "I'm Mr. Fortune, and this is my associate, Ms. De Leon."

Sofia smiled, then took a step forward. "Pardon me, guys, but I noticed the way some of you are dressed. Is this a 1980s day?"

The kids chuckled, and a red-haired girl who was dressed in black and was a Joan Jett look-alike said, "Not officially. Just those of us who are on the dance committee. It's a 1980s theme, and we had a meeting at lunch."

"Yeah," a boy wearing a burnt-orange down vest and blue jeans said. "We thought it would help us be more creative if we dressed this way."

Of course. Marty McFly in *Back to the Future*.

"That's cool," Sofia said. "The dance sounds like it'll be a lot of fun."

She was right. Some of Beau's favorite music was the classic hits from the eighties. Maybe relating to these kids would be a lot easier than he thought it might be.

"I wish Mr. Fortune would have told me he'd dressed the part, too," Sofia said. "Doesn't he remind you of one of the *Caddyshack* characters?"

At that, the class laughed. Before any teenage pandemonium set in, Beau approached the podium. "Ms. De Leon and I want to thank you for being here today. I don't think you'll be disappointed. You might even have fun."

A cough and a couple of groans sounded at the back of the room.

"Let's start with an overview of the course," Sofia said, as she walked to the teacher's desk and picked up the syllabus she and Beau had come up with. She divided the stack and handed half of them to him to pass out.

And just like that, the class began. And so did their teamwork. There might be some underlying differences between them, but for the rest of the hour, neither Beau nor Sofia gave the kids any reason to suspect it.

The late afternoon sun shined bright in the expansive blue sky as Maria and Camila walked along the bike trail at the dog park with Pepe trotting along beside them.

Maria held the leash, although Pepe's collar wasn't connected to it. Sofia had taken the dog to obedience school, which obviously had helped. But Maria suspected Pepe had been born sweet, happy and eager to please his mistress. Or rather, all three of them, since it seemed that they shared custody of their fluffy white fur baby.

Camila glanced at her wristwatch. "Sofia and Beau should be in the middle of their presentation now. I wonder how they're doing."

"I'm sure they're doing great. Sofia worked very hard on it. And Beau did, too. Those students are lucky to have a class like that, even if it only lasts a few weeks. One day it might save them a lot of grief." Maria glanced at her daughter-in-law, who'd become the daughter she'd never had after Ricardo died. "I remember how difficult it was for you after you put your faith in that so-called investment advisor—*el tonto*."

"I'm not sure if he was a fool, Maria. I can't help thinking he was also a thief. Either way, I lost that settlement."

That was true, although Maria knew Camila would have traded every penny of it to have Ricardo back in their lives again. It seemed too cruel, an ugly twist of fate, to lose Ricardo and then have the bulk of the settlement money vanish as well. But Maria shook off the painful past. "He would have been so proud of Sofia."

"Yes, that's true. He adored her. I like to think that he's watching us from above. Our very own guardian angel."

Camila had taken Ricardo's death hard. And while several men had tried to court her in the past, she'd never gotten seriously involved with any of them.

Perhaps that was, at least in part, Maria's fault. She'd moved in with Camila and Sofia nearly twenty years ago, which had worked out nicely for all of them. But maybe that's why Camila avoided bringing another man home. She was always so concerned about others, about their feelings.

Maybe Maria would have to do something about that. At fifty-three, Camila was still a beautiful woman—and too young to live the life of a widow.

Of course, Maria hadn't remarried after her husband died. But that's because Carlos had been the love of her life. And her heart had been buried along with him.

A dog barked, and Pepe stopped. His ears lifted, and he scanned the grassy area. Then he dashed off, something he rarely did.

Camila called him back, but he continued to run toward a tall man walking his dog.

What do you know? That dog looked a lot like M.P., the shepherd mix Beau had been walking when Maria first met him. The man must be the neighbor. Nice-looking, too. In his midfifties, she guessed.

As the dogs met, M.P. tugged on his leash, eager to be turned loose to run and play with his friend.

"I'd better get Pepe," Camila said. She started toward the man and his dog, and Maria fell into step beside her.

"I'm sorry," Camila told the ruggedly handsome man. "Pepe doesn't usually take off like that."

"The dogs are already friends," Maria said. "You must be Beau's neighbor."

"That's right." The man smiled at both women, but his gaze seemed to hover on Camila a bit longer.

Maria glanced at his left hand. No wedding band, but the tan marks on his ring finger claimed there used to be one. Divorced? Widowed? Looking for action by removing the ring?

"My name's Dan Gallagher," he said.

When Camila failed to speak, Maria introduced them both.

"It's nice to meet you," he said.

"I'm sorry about Pepe's interference with your walk."

"No worries. I'm afraid M.P. is still learning his manners, although I think he's going to be a slow learner. He has too much puppy in him, and I'm not sure he'll ever outgrow it." Dan's gaze locked on Camila. "I've seen you before. At the market on South Vine."

Maria glanced at Camila, whose cheeks bore a rosy tint. Hmm. How about that?

"I don't usually shop there," Camila said, "but I'd heard they had a good produce section and thought I'd better try it out. I wasn't disappointed."

"They've got the best meat selection, too." Dan stooped long enough to unleash M.P. and allow the two furry friends to play. "I've been shopping there for years."

"Do you live in that area?" Maria asked.

"Yes. Just a couple blocks away. Right across

the street from Beau. You must already know him since you recognized my dog."

"We had him over for dinner on Saturday," Camila said.

"He's a great guy. And a good neighbor."

Hmm. Maria was familiar with the neighborhood. A church friend lived there. The houses were all fairly modest. Older homes. And certainly not where Maria would expect a Fortune to live. Maybe Sofia was wrong about Beau. Maybe he was more practical than she'd thought. At least, that's the feeling Maria had gotten when she'd met him.

They chatted with Dan for a bit, long enough to learn that he'd served in the Army, was a veteran of Desert Storm and spent time in the military police before retiring ten years ago.

"Thank you for your service," Camila said. "My husband was in the Army when we met, but he didn't make a career of it."

Maria didn't often go into detail about Ricardo's tragic death, but she hoped to make Camila's marital status clear. "He died almost twenty years ago. He was killed by a drunk driver."

"I'm sorry," Dan said. "I lost my wife six months ago. Cancer."

A widower, then. Not a player. Good.

"I'm glad she's no longer suffering," Dan said, "but it's still hard."

"It gets better with time," Camila said.

He shoved his hands into his army camo jacket's pockets. "I sure hope so."

Maria snuck a peek at Camila, then at Dan. Something was going on between them, it seemed. And not just shared grief.

Dan glanced at his wristwatch, then looked at Camila. "Well, I hate to chat and run, but I need to get home. I have an appointment with the cable TV company."

Camila tucked a strand of hair behind her ear, and her eyes sparkled, reminding Maria of the young woman Camila used to be. "It was nice meeting you, Dan. Maybe we'll see you again someday."

"You bet." They exchanged a smile.

They'd definitely meet again, Maria decided. She'd make sure of it. Now she had two romances brewing, and when it came to matchmaking, she was a master.

When the bell rang, ending the presentation, the teenagers began to gather their books and backpacks, but they didn't seem to be in any rush to leave. Sofia took that as a good sign that their project was off to a great start.

The kids hadn't even complained about their first assignment—a research project that required them to come up with a monthly budget for each of the three career scenarios.

"Ms. De Leon?"

Sofia glanced up to see a tall blonde teen approach. "Yes?"

"Can I ask you something?"

"Sure." Sofia gave her a warm smile. "I'm sorry, but I didn't catch your name."

"It's Kelly. Kelly Marshall."

"I'll remember that," she said.

Kelly tucked a long strand of hair behind her ear. "I, um..." She sucked in a deep breath, then slowly blew it out. "I wanted to ask you about the scholarship your company has."

"What would you like to know?"

"My friend is super smart, especially in math. She could become a professor or a stockbroker or even work at NASA. She wants to go to a big university, but her family doesn't have much money. And her dad refuses to let her get a student loan."

"Once she's eighteen," Sofia said, "your friend can take out a loan on her own."

"Yes, she knows that. But he advised her not to because so many people get stuck with huge payments."

That was true. Sofia had to get a couple of them while she was in school, both of which she'd paid off as quickly as she could. "Student loans can be very helpful. But they can also be a big burden when people keep deferring their payments. The interest continues to accrue, and if they're not careful, they can end up with a debt that's twice the size it was. Has she considered checking into other available scholarships?"

"Yes, but they can be pretty competitive. And some of the schools she'd like to attend are really expensive. So I thought I'd get some information on the one you give out."

"Of course. I thought a question like this might come up, so I brought a few applications with me." Sofia walked back to the teacher's desk and reached for her briefcase.

"Can I have two of them?" Kelly asked. "I'm kind of good at math, too. And so far, I'm really liking this class."

Sofia loved being able to help women—both young and old—learn about investing and making wise decisions. "I'm glad to hear that, Kelly. Mr. Fortune and I tried to create a learning environment that would give the students the financial skills that are important to master."

"The Fortune Foundation has some very generous scholarship programs, too," Beau said, walking over after gathering his papers. He'd obviously overheard their conversation. "You and your friend can apply online."

Sofia stifled the urge to roll her eyes. Beau was always trying to one-up her. At least, it sure seemed that way. But she wasn't going to let him have the last word. "De Leon Financial Consulting also offers paid internships during the summer months. Having actual work experience helps tremendously when you graduate."

"I believe the Fortune Foundation offers the same thing," Beau added.

Once again, she felt as if she needed to compete with Mr. Moneybags. And on all levels.

"That's really cool," Kelly said. "I'll talk to my friend and tell her to check it out."

"Good." Sofia handed her the applications.

"Thanks. Can I ask you another question?"

"Sure. What's that?"

"Someone told me that you guys are here because it's some kind of competition."

Sofia glanced at Beau, who seemed to be zeroed in on her—and her response. They were competitors, all right. But no need to air their dirty linen at the school. "Yes, that's true. But I'd like to think we would have done something like this anyway."

"Ms. De Leon's right," Beau said.

When Kelly left and the room was finally empty, Sofia began to gather up her things.

"So what do you think?" Beau asked. "Did we pull it off?"

"I thought it went very well," Sofia said. "Even better than I'd hoped."

"I agree. There's probably another factor at play. Most of them were seniors. And I think they're all looking forward to moving out on their own, so learning to budget is very important."

"So is learning to stash something away for a rainy day. You probably never had to worry about where your next meal was coming from. My grandparents came to this country with nothing, and I'm painfully aware of what it's like to struggle. I'd also venture to say you never had to apply for a student loan or get a job while you were in college. That's why De Leon Financial Consulting created a scholarship fund."

"I admire that."

So he wasn't trying to one-up her? He was actually complimenting her?

"Come on." He took the red box from her and nodded toward the door. "I'll walk you to your car."

All right. He had great manners. She'd have to give him points for that.

She walked along beside him, through the library and outside to the parking lot. She led him to her car, then using the key remote, unlocked the doors.

"Do you want me to put the box in the backseat?" he asked.

"Yes. Thanks." She opened the driver's door, but rather than slide behind the wheel, she remained standing and studied him for a beat. From the moment she'd learned his last name, she'd had him pegged. Yet, right this moment, she wasn't so sure if she'd been entirely right.

After placing the box in the backseat and closing the door, he flashed her a disarming smile, and her tummy took a tumble. Uh-oh. That wasn't good. It wasn't good at all.

She did her best to shake it off. She'd trusted her attraction and her feelings more than once in the past, only to be disappointed, and she'd better keep that in mind.

They might be a team for the next couple of weeks, but after that, the competition was back on.

Chapter Six

Beau waited until Sofia backed her red Lexus out of the parking space and drove away before he walked over to his own vehicle and got behind the wheel.

Moments ago, while they were still in the classroom, an idea had sparked, and he wanted to discuss it with his brother. He'd planned to talk it over in person, but why wait?

As he turned onto the highway, he told Siri to place the call.

Draper picked up on the second ring. "I take it that your class is over. How'd it go?"

"Very well. But I didn't call to talk about that.

I've been thinking about something." Okay, so it was Sofia who'd put the bug in his ear. "Anyway, I want to run it by you."

"Go ahead. I'm listening."

The light ahead turned yellow, and Beau began to brake. "Ever since we moved to Texas, we've gone out of our way to keep a low profile in town. But we might want to rethink that strategy."

"I'm not following you. Are you suggesting we move to Rambling Rose Estates?"

The millionaires who'd moved to town over the last couple of years lived in that gated community. Beau and Draper could certainly afford two separate homes there. "I wouldn't go that far. The house we're renting is fine for now. But we could be doing more for the community."

"The Fortune Foundation has that covered."

"Yes, I know. But I think the Rambling Rose branch of Fortune Investments should do something on its own."

"Like what?"

"Well, for one thing, we could offer scholarships to local high school students. And maybe we should take a good hard look at some of the Rambling Rose charities and choose a couple to support. That would go a long way in gaining community acceptance and respect."

"That's a good idea," Draper said.

The truth was, Beau wanted to help his new

community. He might have started off wanting to get in good with them, but now... Well, he'd come to really care about his neighbors. The town. The high school kids.

"We could start off by making another donation to Jack Radcliffe's Pets2Vets program," Draper said. "It off to a strong start, but there's always room for growth and expansion. Besides, our future brother-in-law would appreciate our regular support."

Their sister Belle would, too. Beau couldn't wait to tell her what he and Draper planned to do.

"Adopting M.P. really helped Dan," Beau said. "It'd be nice to know we were making a contribution to other veterans."

"I agree. Jack's got a great program."

"We need to seriously consider the issues facing people less fortunate than us." Sofia had a point about his family, or at least, the New Orleans branch of it. "We have it a lot easier than most of the Rambling Rose residents. I'd like to help out wherever we can."

"I can't argue with that. Sounds like that Lone Star Best project has been an eye-opener. Thanks again for taking it on for us. I'm sorry you had to shoulder it on your own."

At first, Beau had been a little annoyed at his brother for not playing a more active part in the actual competition, but in all honesty, he was glad to be able to work with Sofia on his own.

"No need to apologize," Beau said. "Business is booming and we can't both be taking time off. Besides, I'm enjoying the project. The kids are great."

"And the competition? With Sofia De Leon?"

Warmth spread through his chest. He couldn't deny his respect for the self-assured woman. Nor his attraction. "So far so good. We make a good team."

While he admired her competitive spirit, he couldn't help wondering if it was a bit over the top. He didn't mind being business competitors, or even competing for the same reward. But after going head-to-head with Gina Vittuli in college, he knew better than to get personally involved with anyone who needed to be first in everything. Damn, Gina had even taken all the fun out of a friendly game of golf.

"Just don't forget you're there to bring home a win for us," Draper said.

"I haven't forgotten." But for the first time, Beau was beginning to wonder if a win really mattered in the long run. Maybe just being nominated was a coup. After all, the Rambling Rose division of Fortune Investments was still so new.

After Draper gave Beau a recap of what went down at the office today, he said, "There's no need for you to come in now."

"Sounds good." Beau ended the call, then turned off the highway at Sage Street and headed home.

He'd no more than reached his house when he spotted Dan standing in his front yard, holding a hose and watering his grass. He was wearing his battered army jacket, a veteran's ball cap shading his weathered face.

When Dan glanced up, Beau waved at him, then pulled into the driveway and parked. As he climbed out of his car, he couldn't help taking note of his own lawn. Time to mow again. And the hedge that ran along the property line, separating Ginny Sanders's yard from his, was getting a bit straggly. He'd have to use a ladder, though. The damn hedge was taller than he was. But he'd seen a ladder in the garage—somewhere amid all the boxes and personal stuff the Dobsons had stored in there.

Draper had suggested that they hire a gardener, but Beau enjoyed working outdoors. Besides, it didn't hurt for the neighbors to see him doing yard work on his own.

Before he could walk to the front door, Dan called out, "You got a minute?"

"Sure." Beau started across the street while the retired Army vet shut off the faucet.

"I met a couple of your friends at the dog park," Dan said.

"What friends?"

"Camila and Maria. Pepe's dog sitters."

The De Leon women. His stomach did a zing. "Oh, yeah?"

"I, uh…" Dan stroked his chin. "You know, I have no interest in dating anyone. At least, I haven't. After Molly died, the thought of getting involved with another woman was the last thing on my mind."

Beau sensed what was coming next. But hell, Camila was a beautiful lady. "It's only natural for you to find another woman attractive."

"I know. It just surprised me, that's all." Dan took off his cap and raked his fingers through his graying hair. "So what do you know about her? She mentioned being a widow, but is she dating anyone?"

"I really don't know much." He knew more about her daughter, although not nearly as much as he'd like. "Camila seems nice. I had dinner at their house the other night. She and Maria sure know how to fix a mouthwatering Mexican meal."

"Yeah, well, if you ever reciprocate, let me know. I grill a mean tri-tip steak."

"You know," Beau said, "I had thought about taking them out to dinner as a thank-you. But I like the idea of having a backyard barbecue."

In fact, he liked it a lot—especially if Sofia joined them. That way, she could see that Beau lived modestly. And that her initial assumption about him and his family was wrong.

On Thursday afternoon, Sofia arrived at Rambling Rose High School at the same time as Beau, and they parked a couple of cars apart, her new Lexus coupe and his Cadillac Escalade separated by a dinged-up Chevy pickup and a shiny new white BMW.

As usual, she'd dressed professionally, this time in a pale green blouse and a modest black skirt and heels. Beau had, too. He wore a white button-down shirt and black trousers.

He closed the distance between them and cast her a smile, his brown eyes sparkling. The man looked damn good, no matter the occasion. But there was no need for him to suspect she'd been assessing his appearance.

So she said, "I can see you came here straight from the office this afternoon, rather than the golf course."

"You pointed out that I was a little too *Caddyshack* on Tuesday, so I thought I'd better follow your lead, although I don't think the kids will care either way."

He was probably right.

"The girls really seemed to like you," he said.

"I got that impression, too." By the end of the class, they seemed to hang on her every word.

She suspected that was due to her insistence that women could enter any field they wanted, even if it was typically dominated by men. As they neared the library entrance, Beau said, "I stopped by your mom's condo on my way here."

He did *what*? Sofia froze in her tracks. "Why? Did you leave something there the other night?"

"No, I invited your mom and grandmother to a barbecue at my house on Sunday afternoon. They said they'd be there. I'd like you to come, too. That is, if you're free."

She was definitely free. But did she want to strike up that kind of relationship with Beau? Not that she hadn't entertained steamy thoughts of them becoming way more than friends, but they'd yet to enter round two of the Lone Star Best competition, and a friendship—or a love affair—between them would throw her off her game.

Damn. Was that part of his plan? Could she trust him to play fairly? She hoped he wasn't up to using any psychological tricks on her.

Either way, she didn't dare let Mama and Abuelita go alone. Who knew what they might say—or let slip—if Sofia wasn't around to control the conversation?

"I don't need an answer right now," Beau said, reminding her that she'd taken a bit too long to think about the invitation.

She wasn't happy about it, but it seemed she'd

been backed into a corner, not only by him but by Mama and Abuelita, too. The traitors. "Sure. I'll come. What can I bring?"

"Not a thing. I've got it all covered. Do you like chicken or steak?"

"Either is fine with me." She continued the short walk to the entrance. "What time?"

"How about four o'clock? We probably won't eat until five. And, if you'd like, you can bring Pepe." Beau opened the door for her, and she walked through it. "I'll give you my address after class."

"All right." She'd actually like to see Beau's neighborhood, to check out how he'd decorated his house. He'd implied that he wasn't all that high-and-mighty, but with the kind of money the Fortunes had, she doubted it.

They'd barely entered the library when they were greeted by Fiona Prather, the school librarian. "Oh, good. You're here. I wanted to catch you before class."

"What's up?" Beau asked.

"I'm not sure if any of the kids told you, but I want to give you a heads-up. There's a school dance on Saturday night. And several students plan to ask if you'd chaperone. Word got out that you two are a super cool couple."

Sofia stiffened. "We're not a couple."

Fiona flushed and placed a hand on her chest. "I'm sorry. The kids seemed to think you were, and you always arrive together, so I just assumed..." Fiona shrugged. "Well, anyway, I'm sorry if I helped that rumor take flight."

"No problem," Beau said. "It was an easy mistake."

Sofia was tempted to argue that point. How had anyone made a jump like that?

"It's actually an honor to be asked," Fiona added. "They're afraid to have their parents chaperone, especially this dance."

"Why?" Sofia asked.

"It's an eighties theme. Their mothers and fathers grew up in the era, and a lot of them have been clamoring to attend. Apparently, the kids are afraid their parents will embarrass them. So they've been carefully choosing the adults who they think are cool."

Beau chuckled and turned to Sofia. "What do you think? Are you available on Saturday night?"

"Let's not get carried away and make assumptions or plans. No one has asked us yet."

"Oh, they'll ask you," Fiona said. "The dance committee has roped in a few of the teachers already, but as far as the school policy goes, they're still short a couple of chaperones."

Sofia glanced at the clock behind the librarian's desk. It was already three, and the bell would be ringing soon. "We'd better go. We need to get ready for day two. Then we'll see what the kids have to say."

As she and Beau walked to the classroom, he gave her a little nudge. The touch of his arm against her shoulder sent heat spiraling through her.

"I don't know how you feel about chaperoning," Beau said. "Normally, I'd try to find a way to get out of something like that. But I like the 1980s theme. And I think it'll be a good way to connect with our students. Besides, I think it'll be fun."

Sofia had to agree. And if truth be told, she didn't have anything else to do on Saturday night. Her friend Carla would be out of town attending some kind of bankers' convention, so other than binge another series on Netflix or play board games with Mama and Abuelita, it would be a quiet evening.

Beau reached the classroom door first and opened it for her. In some ways, she liked his manners. Yet a part of her felt compelled to tell him she didn't need his help. She could open her own doors, thank you very much. But she clamped her mouth shut. Manners went both ways.

"Maybe we should go in costume," he said.

"Seriously?" Sofia hadn't seen that coming. Not from the dashing and stylish Mr. Fortune. "You've got to be kidding, right?"

"No, not at all. Maybe I should dress like Patrick Swayze in *Dirty Dancing*." He reached for her hand, his grip warm and strong, his gaze locked on hers with an intensity that shook her to the core. "'Nobody puts Baby in the corner.'"

Oh, wow. The sexy image knocked her completely off balance, something she had to correct. "Nah. I see you more the Ferris Bueller type."

"Hey!" He returned her smile. "How about you? You'd make a great Madonna or Cyndi Lauper."

Seriously? Her? She waved off what she considered a compliment.

He shrugged. "Or you could wear that red dress you rocked at the Valentine's Day party."

"Sure. And then ask the DJ to play 'Little Red Corvette'?" She shook her head. "I don't think so. If I'm going to be a chaperone, I'm going to dress like one. And I think you should, too."

"Spoilsport." He winked, then shot her a boyish grin.

Damn. The man had a playful side she hadn't seen before, a side that could tempt a career-focused woman to give a life of fun and games a shot.

She bumped him with her elbow in an attempt to change the subject. "The bell is going to ring any second. Let's get organized and ready for the kids."

He gave her a mock salute. "Yes, boss."

Subservience didn't suit him any better than it

did her. Yet a charming manner and that dimpled grin was doing a real number on her. She stole a glance at him, watched him move through the classroom. She couldn't shake the Dirty Dancing image. Of Beau taking her by the hand, just like Johnny did with Baby. Sneaking around, keeping their love affair secret. Spending afternoons in bed.

Oh, for cripes's sake. She'd better shake off thoughts like that. She wasn't about to let any spark of attraction for her teammate sway her. She might be warming to him, but she couldn't let down her guard. This was still a competition, and she couldn't trust whether he was being sincere or trying to get an edge over her.

There could only be one winner, and it was going to be her.

Fiona had been right, Beau decided. Two of the kids on the dance committee entered the classroom first and approached the teacher's desk, where Beau and Sofia had been organizing this afternoon's handouts.

"Excuse us." Kelly Marshall nodded to the teenage boy beside her, a short, stocky ginger with spiked hair and a gray school hoodie, his black designer backpack hanging over his shoulder. "Can we ask you guys something?"

"Sure," Beau said.

Sofia lay down the last stack of papers on the desk. "What's up, Kelly?"

"We, uh…" She hesitated, looked at her stylish, well-dressed friend, then said, "Our committee needs two more chaperones for our dance on Saturday night. And me and Ryan want to know if you'd be willing to do it. It's from seven o'clock until eleven, although I think you'd have to show up thirty minutes early. And maybe hang out until all the kids leave."

Beau glanced at Sofia. "What do you say, Ms. De Leon? Are you available that evening?"

"I'll have to shuffle a few things on my calendar, but yes. I'll help out."

The smile that spread across Kelly's face lit up her green eyes. "Awesome. We really appreciate that." She turned to Ryan. "Give them the instructions."

Ryan reached into his unzipped backpack and pulled out two sheets of paper. "It's pretty simple. All you gotta do is make sure no one does anything stupid. There's even a stupid-things list."

Beau almost laughed at that. He'd done his share of foolish, teenage stunts. "I'll make a note of that."

"Go on." Kelly gave Ryan a nudge. "The bell's gonna ring, and you're going to be late to chemistry. I'll see you after school."

As Kelly plopped down at an empty desk, Ryan

hurried out of the classroom and the other students began to take their seats. Moments later, the bell rang.

Not surprisingly, the second class went just as well—if not better—than the first. The kids had all done their assignment, and whenever Sofia or Beau spoke, most of them listened intently and raised their hands if they had any questions—except for the two lovebirds in the last row who played footsy through the entire lesson. Beau might have called them on it, but they weren't hurting anyone other than themselves.

As the hour progressed, they divided the kids in groups of three to come up with a budget for an assigned situation. Beau noticed that Sofia easily moved from one group to another. And one time, she even pulled up a chair and sat with a couple of girls, whose conversation had drifted to personal issues, like trouble with an overly strict parent and a cheating boyfriend.

Beau heard her say, "Parents. Lovers. Life gets complicated. And it's never simple. Just imagine your mom is ill and you have a two-year-old and a mortgage payment due."

The girls groaned, but they put their heads together and brainstormed a solution.

Beau acted as if he hadn't overheard the group go off topic. Yet at the same time, he admired

Sofia's compassion and the way she handled the issue. He suspected the girls did, too.

When the bell rang and the last student left the room, Beau approached his beautiful teammate. "You would have made a great teacher, Sofia. Or an adolescent psychologist. You've really got a way with teenagers."

"Thanks. It's not a special talent. I guess you could say that I can still remember what it was like to be a teenager—the angst, the drama and all that. But I'm old enough to have learned a few things along the way."

"No, you have a gift."

She waved him off but looked pleased with the comment. Then she began to pack up her red box.

He liked seeing her drop her competitive edge once in a while.

"You seem to have a nice connection with the boys, too," she said.

"Maybe I remember doing all those stupid things on the list Ryan gave me, so I don't judge or preach."

"I don't believe it," Sofia said. "What did you do?"

"I accidentally—on purpose—locked the coach's keys in his pickup. Then there was the Vaseline on the coach's doorknobs. And the fake snake in the locker room shower."

Sofia laughed. "You had it in for that poor man, but is that all you got?"

He shrugged. No, he had a few more. But no need for her to think he was a hellion. "Yeah, that's about it." He nodded toward the door. "Come on. I'll walk you to your car."

Sofia glanced at the clock on the wall. "I'll have to pass. I told Fiona I'd have a cup of coffee with her after school."

Beau hadn't seen that coming. Was she gathering some sort of inside information to get a competitive edge? Maybe he ought to invite himself to join in.

But he thought better of it. "No worries. I'll see you on Saturday night."

And again on Sunday.

On the drive to the office, Beau called his neighbor. "Hey, Dan. We're on for that barbecue on Sunday."

"And all three ladies will be there?" Dan asked.

"Yes. I'll pick up the tri-tip and have it at my house. You can come over whenever you want to marinate it. Or whatever you plan to do. I'm not that great of a cook, unless we have a crawfish boil." He also figured he'd call Provisions, his favorite local restaurant, and order some side dishes and dessert.

Beau didn't usually have company. And he'd never had anyone over to the rental house he and

Draper shared. But that didn't matter. He was looking forward to seeing Sofia two days in a row—the
dance on Saturday night, followed by the barbecue in his backyard.

There was no telling what the weekend would
bring, but he couldn't help thinking…

Wait a sec. Was he letting down his guard?

He smiled to himself. Yeah, maybe so.

But did that really matter?

Chapter Seven

Beau hadn't been kidding when he'd suggested that he and Sofia dress according to the eighties theme, even though he didn't expect her to. He'd gone shopping on Thursday evening and found a brown leather flight jacket, a white T-shirt and a pair of faded jeans—a replica of the outfit Pete "Maverick" Mitchell, the lead character in *Top Gun*, had worn. He even picked up a pair of classic aviator sunglasses to wear when he made his grand entrance. Then he drove to the high school for the chaperone gig.

The dance committee had done one heck of a job decorating the gymnasium with the eighties theme. A variety of movie posters representing the era—like *St. Elmo's Fire*, *Ferris Bueller's Day Off* and *Romancing the Stone*—had been plastered all over the walls, and several Brat Pack movies played silently on monitors set up throughout the gym.

The DJ played hits from the eighties, and the kids danced to tracks by Michael Jackson, Bon Jovi, Cyndi Lauper and many more.

Beau couldn't help swaying to the beat. Were chaperones allowed to dance? Nah. That wouldn't be cool.

The kids all sported outfits and hairstyles from that decade, and Beau could almost imagine being an extra during the school dance scene in one of his favorite 80s movies. He wouldn't be surprised to see a young Molly Ringwald or Anthony Michael Hall walk by.

But there was one person Beau wanted most to see. He scanned the gymnasium, past the dance floor and spotted Sofia chatting with a couple of girls from their class, one of whom was Kelly.

Sofia had nixed dressing in costume. Instead, she had on that red dress she'd worn to the Valentine's Day party at the Hotel Fortune.

Damn, if she wasn't the prettiest chaperone he'd ever seen—or any woman, for that matter, in person or on the screen.

Kelly whispered something in Sofia's ear, and

Sofia bit her lip, frowned, then smiled and nodded. Kelly clapped her hands, gave a little jump, then dashed toward the partygoers crowded around the disc jockey.

What was that all about?

"Hi, Beau."

At the raised yet soft sound of a woman's voice, he tore his gaze from Sofia and turned to Ginny Sanders, his quiet-spoken neighbor who taught English lit at the high school. He smiled. "Hey, Ginny. I see they roped you into chaperoning, too."

"Yes, they did," the petite brunette said. "I heard you were teaching a special, short-term class at the school, but I'm surprised to see you here."

Beau shrugged. "The dance committee asked me and Sofia, and I figured, why not?" He gestured around the gym. "They did a great job with the decorations, didn't they?"

"Definitely. This reminds me of the school dance in *Sixteen Candles*."

"Me, too," he said. "That was a great movie. It was on television the other night, and I watched it again."

Ginny smiled, then tucked a long strand of brown hair behind her ear. She stood beside him and seemed to be at a loss for words, yet Beau wasn't sure what to say, either. Unlike other neighbors on the block, he rarely talked to Ginny. He and Dan had hit it off right away, and he often chatted with Joey and Samantha Billings, whose family lived next door. But his conversations with Ginny had been few and far between. He knew so very little about her that it made small talk difficult. But maybe he could remedy that with a couple of questions.

"I notice that you spend a lot of time painting on your front porch," he said.

"It's something I try to do each day. I had a double major in college—studio art because I love to paint and English lit so I could actually earn a living."

"Good plan."

"I, uh, don't see much of your brother Draper. He seems to come and go a lot."

"He keeps busy." Draper wasn't one to stick close to the house. Not that Beau was a homebody. He was just more guarded and driven than his brother, and he tended to notice details. On the other hand, Draper was fast moving, a big-idea man. Their differences worked well for them in business, and it even seemed to deepen their brotherly bond.

"What keeps him so busy?" Ginny asked.

"Work," Beau said. "As well as pleasure."

Draper liked fancy cars and the ladies. Of course, Beau liked women as much as his brother, but when he dated, he tended to stick with the same woman for a while. On the other hand, Draper wasn't the kind to make a serious commitment.

"Does he play sports?" Ginny asked. "Or have any hobbies?"

Uh-oh. He was beginning to wonder if she had a little crush on Draper, which was too bad. As nice as she was, Ginny Sanders wasn't Draper's type. She was Prius, and Draper was Ferrari.

"He plays golf and tennis," Beau said. "When he finds time." Then, to steer the subject away from his brother, he added, "How about you?"

"I've played tennis before, and I ride horses, but I'd much rather paint."

"I figured." He offered her a smile. "Because I see you on your porch a lot."

"I…was painting last Saturday, and I spotted a Porsche parked in your driveway. The woman who got out looked a lot like Ines Bartholomew, the field reporter on *Entertainment Right Now*."

Ines was also Miss Texas and the fourth runner up to Miss USA. "It was her. She's…Draper's friend."

"I thought so," Ginny said.

Fortunately, Beau spotted Sofia standing off to the side of the refreshment table. "If you'll excuse me, I'd better make sure none of the kids has spiked the punch bowl."

As he stepped away, she said, "There's no punch. They're serving soda in cans."

He continued toward Sofia, hoping that Ginny would think her comment was lost in the sound of the music, chatter and laughter. How could he tell Ginny that she wasn't his brother's type? It might hurt her feelings. Then again, she'd probably already figured that out.

Moments later, he was at Sofia's side. "Having fun?"

"Yes, although it's a little weird. I'd never want to go back to my high school days, but this evening, I can't help wishing I was seventeen again."

"I know what you mean. This setting kind of makes me wish I was a kid again too, but just for tonight." Beau had fond memories of his teen years, but he'd moved beyond those days.

Still, it wasn't just the setting, the mood and the music that made him feel nostalgic and gave him an unexpected thrill tonight. It was Sofia.

"Oh, I nearly forgot," she said. "My grandmother wants to know what she can bring to the barbecue at your house tomorrow."

"She doesn't have to bring anything."

"I know that. But she insists."

He'd taken wine to her house, but he didn't want to ask her to bring something like that. "How about her homemade guacamole and salsa *fresca*? I'll have the tortilla chips."

"Are you making Mexican food?"

"Absolutely not. Don't get me wrong. I love

it, but I wouldn't even try to compete with your abuelita. She makes the best I've ever had."

Sofia smiled, and her brown eyes sparkled. "I'll tell her you said that."

Before Beau could reply, Kelly and two other girls hurried up to Sofia.

"It's time," Kelly said.

"Will you excuse me?" Sofia asked Beau. "But don't go anywhere."

"Sure." If she was coming back, he'd wait for her.

Sofia, along with three of the high school girls, each wearing a red dress, walked to the center of the dance floor.

"We have a special request," the DJ announced. "Will you all clear the dance floor?"

The kids moved to the sides, while Sofia and the girls remained in the center.

The DJ started the music, and Beau immediately recognized "The Lady in Red." The three girls sauntered off to find a dance partner, and his gaze locked on Sofia as she glided his way. She reached out her hand in silent invitation, and he took it. Then she led him onto the dance floor, where she slipped into his arms. They began to dance, face-to-face at first, then cheek to cheek.

Her perfume, something light and floral, drove him to distraction—in the nicest way. She felt warm against his body, and they moved as though they'd danced together for years. He didn't want the music to end. When it did, they lingered a moment, their eyes locked on each other. It seemed as if they were the only couple on the dance floor, the only ones in the room. Her lips parted. He felt compelled to kiss her in the worst way, and if he was reading her silent gaze correctly, she wasn't likely to object. Only trouble was, this was the wrong place and the wrong time.

He slowly lowered his arms, releasing her from his embrace. His heartbeat pounded so hard he could scarcely hear the teen whistles, whoops and applause. As several corner lights turned on, Sofia flushed a shade lighter than her dress.

"I'm sorry," he said, not sure what else to say.

"For what?" She looked at him with those soulful brown eyes, then she blinked and took a step back. "Thanks for going along with this. It was Kelly's idea. When she saw what I was wearing, she begged me to join in. I was afraid you might balk or feel awkward."

Beau hadn't felt any such thing. He'd been flattered at first. And mesmerized later.

"How could I resist?" he asked.

Her breath hitched, but she didn't respond. Not right away. Instead, she nodded toward the refreshment table. "I'd better go back to my post."

He reluctantly agreed but stealthily watched Sofia for the rest of the night. If they were alone after the dance, he wasn't sure if he could stop himself from kissing her.

Sofia couldn't wait to walk off the dance floor and get back to the refreshment table where she could stand off to the side and out of the spotlight. She needed a minute or two to cool down. She could still feel the warmth of Beau's arms around her while they swayed to the music, her cheek on his. He'd shaved before arriving tonight. She was sure of it because of the pleasant, alluring scent of his aftershave—an earthy but clean smell that dazzled her. Yet there was a soft, tantalizing roughness to his skin that put her senses on high alert.

As the music played, their hearts had beat together to the rhythm of the romantic song. And for those few brief minutes while they danced, she'd forgotten that there were more than a hundred teenagers looking on, watching them.

"Hey," Kelly said, drawing Sofia from her thoughts. "Thanks for being such a good sport, Ms. De Leon."

"You're welcome. It's been a while since I danced, so it was fun." But dancing with Beau had been more than pleasurable or entertaining. It had been heart-strumming, hormone-swirling and thought-provoking.

"You and Mr. Fortune make a good couple," Kelly said. "Are you guys a thing?"

"Oh, no. We aren't." They were turning into something other than competitors, though, even if Sofia had no idea what it was.

The truth was, Sofia had gotten so caught up in the music and the festive atmosphere that she'd wanted to dance, and her options for a partner had been limited.

Who else could she have taken out on the dance floor? Mr. Conway, the earth science teacher, or Mr. Taylor, who taught auto shop for years? Both were chaperones this evening—and old enough to be her father. So Beau had been the sole choice. Only trouble was, dancing with him had stirred up feelings that were better left buried.

Beau seemed to steer clear of her for the rest of the evening, which was probably for the best. But after most of the teenagers had filed out of the gym, leaving the cleanup committee to work along with a couple of janitors, Beau finally approached her.

"We survived," he said.

"Yes, we did." She offered him a smile.

"It wasn't so bad. Was it?"

"Not in the least. I actually had a good time."

"So did I." His gaze locked on hers, and there it went again. The tingle in her belly. The elevated heart rate. The hormonal buzz. "You're a good dancer."

"Thanks. So are you."

"Oh, yeah?" His smile dimpled his cheeks and lit his eyes. "My mom will be happy to know those cotillion classes she made me attend when I was a kid weren't a waste."

The fact that Sofia had never had a dance lesson in her life, let alone any classes that taught social graces, didn't escape her. But right this minute, standing in the midst of a nearly empty gymnasium, it didn't seem to matter. Not in the least.

Whew. It was getting warm in here.

"Come on," he said. "I'll walk you to your car."

Good idea. When he offered his arm, she took it and let him escort her out of the gym. It would be nice to get outside in the evening air. Maybe then she'd feel more like herself and less like an awkward teenager.

Once they'd left the gym, she sucked in a cool, refreshing breath. That was better.

He slowed to a stop, yet she still clung to his arm. "The sky sure is pretty tonight."

She glanced up and saw a million tiny stars shining overhead and a nearly full moon. "You're right." But it was more than that sight that made the evening special.

They continued to walk to the parking lot, their shoulders brushing, his warmth seeping deep into her bones. There were only a few cars left, so hers was easy to find, and his wasn't far away.

"Thanks for walking me out." With a bit of reluctance, she released his arm.

"My pleasure."

She faced the car, and with the remote in her purse, all she had to do was open the driver's door, but for some dumb reason, she turned to face him. She wasn't sure what she was expecting—more small talk, a little verbal banter... Funny thing, though. She wasn't actually up for either.

He placed his hand on her jaw, and her breath caught. Damned if he wasn't going to kiss her. Her heart skipped, then took off like a shot. His thumb brushed across her cheek, and her lips parted.

Now was the time to stop him, to tell him this was a bad idea. A very bad one. But she didn't do a blasted thing other than tingle in the shimmering moonlight.

He lowered his lips to hers. Even if her derriere hadn't been pressed against the car door, she still wouldn't have stepped away, wouldn't have stopped him. Instead, she slipped her arms around his neck and drew him into a kiss.

His lips were soft yet demanding. His breath was cool and refreshing, but at the same time, hot and arousing. The kiss intensified until they were making out like a couple of teenagers on a hormone high.

Teenagers. The high school.

They were supposed to be chaperones, for goodness' sake. What if someone saw them?

And they were also competitors. What in the hell was she doing?

Sofia drew her mouth from his, ending the kiss. "I, uh, don't know what we were thinking. We can't do this."

"We can't undo it, either," he said. "But if this is what you want…"

It wasn't. Not right this minute. She had too much to risk. Too much to lose. And she wasn't about to pursue that conversation any further. "Let's forget it happened."

"That's not likely."

Right. She certainly wasn't going to forget a kiss like that. But she darn sure couldn't let it happen again.

"Sofia," he said, easing forward, his gaze filled with compassion.

But she didn't need his sympathy or his understanding. Not when she didn't know what she needed. She placed a firm hand on his chest. "No. Stop. Please stop. I meant what I said. This isn't right. We can't do this."

He stared at her as if this was a first for him. And it probably was. Not many women would tell a gorgeous, wealthy man who could turn a woman inside out with his kiss to back off.

He took an abrupt step back. With raised hands, he said, "I'm sorry."

"No worries." Sofia turned and opened the driver's door. "I need to go."

"Will I see you tomorrow?" he asked.

Oh, yeah. His house. The barbecue. When she made a commitment, she kept it—something she'd learned from her mother and grandmother, both of whom would be in attendance.

"Yes," she said, trying to sound nonchalant and maintain her no-worries response. "What time again?"

"Four o'clock."

"Got it." Then she slid behind the wheel and quickly drove out of the lot.

At the stop sign, she glanced in her rearview mirror. Beau remained rooted to the same spot, watching her—and looking stunned.

He'd just have to put that kiss behind him. That's what she planned to do.

Only trouble was, she'd liked kissing him way too much. But falling for him would be the biggest mistake of her life.

Beau Fortune might seem like a nice guy, but he was mega rich and too attractive for his own good. The two of them were clearly unsuited. They were competitors and opposites in so many ways.

Yet, like it or not, Sofia was going to see him again tomorrow. And as much as she'd like to tell him something unexpected had come up, it was too late.

Chapter Eight

Beau waited until Sofia had driven away, then he got into his car and headed home. He'd thought about kissing her good-night all evening, and he hadn't been disappointed. She'd even taken the lead. Hadn't she? Or had he forced himself on her? Nah. It was mutual.

He'd never had such an arousing kiss—and it had been worth the wait.

Then, all of a sudden—pow! She'd blindsided him.

Back off?

Pretend it hadn't happened? Not a chance. The feel of her in his arms, the stirring scent of her perfume, the way her tongue had sought his, tasting, mating…

He stewed about it and her rejection all the way home.

When he pulled into his driveway, the house was dark, which meant Draper wasn't home yet. After parking, he got out of his SUV and started up the walkway. The motion detector kicked on, lighting his way to the front door and revealing a small brown box on the porch. Draper must have ordered something online. Then again, it could be for Beau, although, off the top of his head, he couldn't remember doing so lately. Right now, all he could think about was Sofia—and the kiss that had rocked his world—and knocked him off balance.

He reached for his key and unlocked the door. After turning on the living room lamp, he went back outside for the box and carried it into the house. Oddly enough, it was addressed only to FORTUNE—no first name, although a dark smudge in front of the F might have been an initial. And as luck would have it, there wasn't a return label.

That was odd. It had to be something for Draper. So he put it on the hall console with the other unopened mail—mostly junk, since they had all bills and anything of importance sent to the office. Then he went into the living room and slumped into a chair, recalling the night's events. Sofia really had him stumped.

He'd been cautious with his dates in the past. His oldest brother Austin had had a disastrous first marriage. He'd been swept off his feet by a woman who was the daughter of two convicted con artists. And it soon became clear that she'd married him for his money. The divorce had cost Austin—and their family who bailed him out—a lot of money.

As a result, Beau had tried to sidestep anyone who hoped to marry a Fortune for the wrong reason, and so far, he'd been successful. But he hadn't realized a potential wife might *resent* the family's wealth and status.

Before he could give it any more thought, his cell phone rang. He checked the display screen and spotted Dan's name. He wasn't going to cancel, was he? If so, Beau would have to man the grill himself.

"Hey, Dan. You're up late."

"I was watching an old World War II flick on TV and decided to turn in for the night. When I was shutting the blinds, I noticed your car was in the driveway. How was the dance?"

"Okay, I guess. The kids seemed to have a great time. And being a chaperone wasn't that hard."

"What about Sofia?" Dan asked. "Did she make it through the evening unscathed?"

"I hope so." In fact, he knew she had, as far as

the dance went. But after they'd kissed in the parking lot, all bets were off.

"You didn't get a chance to talk to her at the dance?"

Beau sucked in a deep breath, then blew it out. "Yeah, we talked. And after I kissed her goodnight, things went sideways."

"You kissed her? What do you mean, *sideways*?"

"She seemed to really be into it. Then she put a stop to it and said it should have never happened. And when I tried to ease her mind, she pretty much told me to back off."

There was a pause, then Dan said, "Ouch."

"Yeah. But that kiss was out of this world. At least, I thought we both enjoyed it. But she wants to pretend it didn't happen. So maybe I read her wrong."

"Come on, man. You can't tell when a woman enjoys a kiss?"

"I thought I could. I always have."

"Regardless," Dan said, "she put you in your place. Don't risk losing that competition."

No way. He intended to win. And so did Sofia.

His gut clenched. She certainly had a competitive nature. Was hers as strong as his former college girlfriend's? Gina had gone out of her way to be the best at everything—and not just at golf.

The woman always had to have the last word, even when she knew darn well she'd lost the argument.

"You don't want Sofia to file a complaint," Dan added. "Best to move on, kid."

"Yeah, maybe you're right." But Sofia was different from Gina.

And from other women he'd dated. She was smarter. Prettier. Harder to read. And she wasn't one to be taken lightly. But he wasn't going to make a decision now. He'd have to wait and see how tomorrow went.

"Did you call just to ask about the dance?" Beau asked.

"No, I wanted to see if there was anything you needed me to do for the barbecue tomorrow. But now I'm wondering if it's still on."

"As far as I know, it is. At least, she said she'd be here."

"That's a good sign."

Was it?

"She might bring Pepe," Beau said. "If she does, you can bring M.P."

"We'll see how he's behaving," Dan said. "Why don't you come over early? We'll have a Corona before the ladies arrive."

"Sounds good."

Beau ended the call and went into the bathroom to take a shower. He was looking forward to seeing Sofia again, but it might be awkward. No, it would definitely be awkward. It'd be helpful to have another guy around, just in case he needed backup.

Dan had been right, though. If Sofia didn't want that kind of relationship with him, he'd have to move on. But he couldn't help hoping that she would have a change of heart.

On Sunday morning, Beau woke to the sound of the Billings kids playing ball in the street. He cracked an eye and looked at the clock on the bureau. Seven fifteen? Damn.

He tried going back to sleep, but he didn't have any luck. So he rolled out of bed and headed for the kitchen. A cup of coffee was in order. He'd called Provisions yesterday and ordered salads and a cheesecake for the barbecue. He'd have to pick it up early this afternoon, but other than that, there wasn't much to do—except mow the backyard and get ready for company.

After the coffee brewed, he poured himself a cup and carried it into the living room, where he plopped down on the leather sofa and reached for the remote. May as well catch the top news story and check the weather.

Nothing noteworthy in the headlines, but the weatherman announced an unexpected storm was moving in, although it wasn't supposed to hit until nightfall. That shouldn't affect the barbecue. Still, if they had to make a change in plans, they could eat indoors.

Moments later, Draper entered the room, his light brown hair damp from the shower and a white towel wrapped around his waist. "Good morning."

"Hey." Beau turned off the TV. "Did those little rug rats wake you up, too?"

"No. I set the alarm." Draper walked to the living room window, opened the shutters and peered into the street. "But they're up and at 'em early."

"I didn't hear you come in," Beau said. "Late night?"

"You can say that again." Draper stretched and rolled his shoulders, then turned away from the window. "Hank Elliot, one of my clients, invited me to a poker game at his house, and it went into overtime."

Beau took a sip of coffee. "You come out ahead?"

"I didn't win much money, but I met some great guys. And I gained us another account. Grant Lewis, who just sold his start-up for mega bucks and needs to figure out what to do with all the cash."

"Good deal."

That's how big clients were found. Late-night poker games, a round of golf. Sofia would be hard-pressed to find opportunities like that. It wasn't fair, but it also wasn't his fault for getting breaks like that.

Beau lifted his mug, then paused, mid sip. Winning the competition would mean so much more to her than to him. Could he put his competitive nature aside and let her prevail? Maybe, but something told him, unlike Gina, Sofia wouldn't want to win that way.

He nodded toward the kitchen. "I just brewed a pot of coffee."

"Thanks. I can sure use a caffeine boost."

"You got plans today?" Beau asked.

"Ray Jennings invited me to brunch at his country club. He wants us to join, and he's going to show me around."

Another opportunity to find mega investors. "We probably ought to join, Draper."

"I know. I heard the buy-in fee for that club is over a hundred grand."

Not a stretch for the Fortune brothers. But it might be tough for someone like Sofia to get access to a place like that.

"I'll check it out," Draper said. "But I have a feeling he also intends to introduce me to his daughter."

"The missionary?" Beau asked. So not his brother's type.

"No, I think this one is an archaeologist."

Beau chuckled. "If you need an excuse to cut out early, I'm having a barbecue this afternoon. You're more than welcome to join us."

"Who's coming?"

"Sofia De Leon, her mother and grandmother. Dan's going to grill tri-tip. I think he's interested in Sofia's mom."

"That's a good sign. I'm glad to hear he's not still moping around."

Beau nodded. "Poor guy's been pretty lost."

Draper headed for the kitchen and returned with a cup of coffee. "I'm not sure when I'll be home, but I'd like to meet the woman who's caught your eye."

"Actually, she isn't interested in me." Beau went on to explain his dilemma. "It's weird. I've been cautious about dating anyone interested in the Fortune's wealth and connections—thanks to Austin's divorce, not to mention Gina's attempt to convince me to sponsor her on the LPGA golf circuit since I was what she'd referred to as a trust fund baby. But I hadn't expected someone to be turned off by the family name."

"Austin's experience was a nightmare. And it taught us all a harsh lesson—to trust but verify everyone's story. I'm just glad he's finally put it behind him."

Yeah, but it hadn't been easy. It had taken years for their older brother to pay back his family and amass his own fortune. Now he was happily re-married to Felicity Schafer, his former personal assistant. But Austin's first wife and her family had taught Beau to be cautious about relationships since some people were only interested in the Fortune's wealth and connections.

Draper glanced at the clock on the mantel. "I'd better get dressed. I don't want to be late."

"I forgot to tell you," Beau said. "A package arrived for you."

Draper furrowed his brow. "I don't remember ordering anything. I'll check it out when I get home."

"All right. I'm taking off, too." Beau snatched his car remote from the counter. "I'll see you later."

"Yes, you will." Draper flashed him a grin. "I want to meet the woman who told you to back off."

"Don't forget the bro-code."

Draper laughed. "Don't worry. I won't. You saw her first."

"Don't drag in too late this afternoon. Sofia might make it an early evening."

"Why would she cut out early?"

"The woman's unpredictable."

"I hate to tell you, brother, but they all are. That's what makes them so fun—and keeps us on our toes." Draper laughed as he left the room.

If that was true, Sofia had practically turned Beau into a spinning atom. Oh, well. He might as well get a move on, too. The mower was out of gas. And that lawn wasn't going to trim itself. He sighed. While he was at it, he'd better check the propane. He should have done it yesterday, but thanks to Sofia, he'd been thrown way off his game.

"Come on, Pepe." Sofia took the leash, locked up her condo, then took the dog out to the car. She made the quick, two-block drive to pick up Mama and Abuelita, who were standing outside, ready to go. At least, someone was looking forward to having dinner at Beau's.

After the women carefully placed the appetizers in the trunk, they got into the car and allowed the GPS to guide them to Beau's house.

Sofia had assumed he and his brother lived at Rambling Rose Estates, the newer gated community, where most of the wealthy residents had purchased homes over the last few years. But that's not where she was heading.

"Are you sure you got the address right?" Sofia asked her mother.

"Yes. And Mr. Gallagher confirmed it when we ran into him at the park."

"It's on the right side of the street," Abuelita said. "Just a few houses down."

Sofia parked along the curb, in the shade of an elm tree, just as a boy on a skateboard zipped by, followed by a girl wearing rollerblades.

"What?" Mama gasped. "No helmets?"

Before Sofia could respond, a woman rushed

out of the house and shouted to the kids. "Get back here! You know the safety rules. Not without knee pads and helmets."

"Oh, thank goodness," Mama said.

Sofia's mother had been very protective—sometimes it had seemed that she was overly so. But she was right. Accidents happened quickly, as Papa's had.

"Looks like this is it," Sofia said, although she still found it hard to believe that the Fortune brothers lived here, in a small, older home in need of fresh paint. Not that there was anything wrong with the house or the neighborhood.

She got out of the car just as a cool breeze kicked up and the leaves rustled in the trees. She glanced at the sky. Dark clouds had begun to gather and it smelled like rain.

"Looks like a storm is brewing," she said. "Maybe they'll have to postpone the barbecue."

"Don't be silly," Abuelita said. "We can just move inside. I'll be happy to cook or help. I've learned to be flexible. And you should, too."

No doubt. The darkening sky wasn't the only thing that gave Sofia an ominous vibe. She had to face Beau after last night's kiss, after she told him to back off. She'd been a little harsh, but the kiss had been too hot for her comfort, especially if she wanted to keep her wits about her.

She probably could have handled it better, but at

least, she didn't have to worry about that happening again, especially with her mother and grandmother looking on.

"Sofia," Mama said. "You'll have to take Pepe's leash. I'm going to help carry in the appetizers."

Abuelita had not only made a double batch of salsa *fresca* and guacamole, she'd also insisted upon bringing her warm bean-and-cheese dip. But that was Abuelita—always going above and beyond, especially when she got into the kitchen.

"Just remember," Sofia said softly, "we're only staying until after we help with the dinner dishes."

Abuelita winked at Mama, who wore a Cheshire grin.

Sofia rolled her eyes. "No shenanigans. You promised." She picked up the end of Pepe's leash. "Come on. Let's get this over with."

Pepe wagged his tail, then jumped out of the car, eager to embark on whatever adventure the women had started. As they walked along the sidewalk, she wondered why Beau's car wasn't parked in the garage. She supposed it was none of her business. A wet droplet landed on her forehead. Then another. Great. It was already starting to rain.

When they reached the front porch, Abuelita stopped and said, "Beau sure keeps a nice yard."

Sofia rang the doorbell. "I just hope this dinner doesn't go into overtime. I have a lot to do when I get home."

"Don't be a party popper," Abuelita said.

"It's *party pooper*." Sofia blew out a soft sigh. "Like I said, I have things to do."

To Sofia's surprise, instead of Beau, an older man opened the door. "Hello, ladies. It's nice to see you again, Camila. Maria."

They'd already met?

His smile was warm, friendly and a bit shy. He turned to Sofia. "I'm Dan Gallagher, Beau's neighbor." He reached out a work-roughened hand. "You must be Sofia."

She took it. "Yes, I am. It's nice to meet you."

Dan glanced down at the dog on the leash. "I'm glad you brought Pepe. M.P. will be glad to see him. He's in the backyard, watching Beau light the grill."

Before anyone could reply, M.P. came bounding through the house, gave a happy bark and greeted Pepe like a long-lost brother. And in that moment, Pepe seemed to forget everything he'd learned in that obedience class they took at Paws and Claws.

Great. Here they were, like one happy family— fur babies included. She couldn't shake the feeling that she'd just entered a big-top circus.

Pepe lunged forward, eager to play, but she held him steady. "Settle down. You know better than that, Pepe. Come back here."

The dog hesitated for a moment, then reluctantly complied.

Dan stepped aside, allowing them into the small, modest, but clean and tidy living room. He reached for the hot dish Mama held. "Can I take that for you, Camila?"

"Sure. Thank you." Mama handed it to him, along with the potholders. "It's still warm, so be careful."

Wait. What…? Was Mama blushing?

"I'll handle it with care," he said. "Let's put it on the coffee table. Here." He put the potholders on the table, then placed the hot dish on top.

Abuelita set her two bowls on the table, too.

"Now, that looks mighty tasty," Dan said. "Can I get you a drink? Wine, beer, water?"

"Wine for me," Abuelita said.

"I'll have the same. Thank you, Dan." Mama smiled shyly.

And would you look at that? He blushed right back at her, then glanced at Sofia.

"Just water for me." She wasn't about to have anything alcoholic. She'd better keep her wits about her, because the circus was about to begin, and she might find herself walking with Beau on the high wire.

"Got it," Dan said. "Please. Make yourselves comfortable. I'll tell Beau you're here. And I'll be back in a flash."

Mama took a seat on the leather sofa, leaving room for Sofia and Abuelita. But Sofia opted for one of two easy chairs. Although, when she sat down, she didn't feel the least bit easy. Or comfortable. But at least, she'd created some distance. No one would wedge beside her. And she could keep a close eye on Mama.

Where had she met Beau's neighbor? At the dog park? Probably, but why hadn't anyone mentioned it? Beau certainly hadn't.

Abuelita took a moment to scan the living room. "Beau lives here with his brother?"

"Yes," Sofia said.

"It's clean for two bachelors."

Abuelita had a point. They must have a housekeeper. Sofia took a moment to study the room, too. The house was fairly simple. The furniture was nice—but not very expensive, which was good. She'd feel a little uncomfortable sitting in a fancy house and trying to make conversation with people who were rich and famous—like Beau and Draper Fortune.

Speak of the devil…

Beau entered the room wearing a polo shirt and a pair of jeans that appeared to be a designer brand. "Welcome, ladies." He smiled at Sofia. "Thanks for coming. You look nice."

Sofia's gaze drifted from his eyes to his lips, and she stiffened. She couldn't possibly look nice. She had to look the way she felt—uneasy. But she managed a thank-you, then folded her arms and crossed her legs.

Needless to say, the evening was starting out awkwardly. Too bad she was only drinking water. If she'd have a glass or two of wine, she might sit back, relax and enjoy the company, rather than perch on the edge of the easy chair, twisted in a knot and clutching a bottle of chilled water. She fought a frown—one that bordered on impolite. *Get a grip, girl. It was only a kiss.*

"I'm sorry I wasn't here to greet you at the door," Beau said. "I was getting things ready in the kitchen." He glanced at Pepe, who sat quietly at Sofia's feet while M.P. kept nudging him with his nose, tempting him to run amok. "I thought the dogs would have fun playing in the yard. And I'd planned for us to eat outside, but it looks like we'll all have to stay indoors."

"No matter," Abuelita said. "We're just happy to be here and looking forward to getting to know you better."

Speak for yourself, Sofia thought, but she clamped her lips together.

Abuelita's gaze locked on Sofia, her eyes narrowing as if scolding a naughty child. "Aren't we, *mija*?"

Okay, so a woman never grew too old to be admonished by her grandmother. Sofia managed a smile. "Yes, that's right. Thank you for inviting us."

"Glad you're here. Thanks for braving the weather."

Sofia had braved more than the weather, but she may as well make the best of it.

"So, tell me," Abuelita said. "Why did you and your brother leave your father's company and move to Rambling Rose?"

Nothing like jumping right into what must be a carefully planned and strategically launched interrogation, although Sofia had to admit, she was curious about the man and where he came from.

"We're still very much a part of the family business," Beau said. "We opened a new branch of Fortune Investments here. The location is perfect. It's halfway between Austin and Houston."

"That's good," Abuelita said. "It's nice to see close families. How many of your siblings live here, in Rambling Rose?"

"Three of us. My brother Draper, my sister Belle and me. Nolan lives in Austin with his wife Lizzie and their baby. Georgia works for the home office in New Orleans. And Savannah has a doctorate and does science research."

He certainly had a lot of siblings, Sofia thought. A kid could get lost in a crowd like that. Of course, they'd never be lonely.

"Sofia," Abuelita said, "why don't you let poor

Pepe play with his friend? It's hard to see him sitting there, so stiff and sad."

She was holding on to him because she didn't want him to create a ruckus, but Abuelita was right. It wasn't fair that one dog remain tethered while the other was free to run and play.

"Do you mind?" she asked Beau.

"Not at all. I think we should all kick back and have fun."

He'd pointed that remark at her, and if truth be told, she didn't feel the least bit relaxed or playful, but why punish Pepe? She unhooked his leash, and the two dogs took off, running in circles like a couple of litter mates having a family reunion.

Beau flashed a dazzling smile that tempted her to let down her guard, to loosen her tether and play.

But the Fortunes and De Leons couldn't be any more different from one another. And it was best that Sofia remember that.

"I'd better check on the meat," Beau said. "I don't want it to get dried out."

"And I'll help you set out the side dishes," Dan said.

When the men left the room, Mama leaned forward and lowered her voice. "Sofia, what's the matter? You're so tense. You look ready to snap."

"You've hardly smiled at all," Abuelita said. "That's not like you. Where are your manners, *mija*? We're guests at this house. And those gentleman have been nothing but nice."

It had been years since Sofia had been scolded by either woman, and she didn't like the way it felt now. She sighed. She couldn't offer any defense. They were right.

If she and Beau were going to continue to work together at the high school, she'd have to get over her discomfort.

"Will you excuse me?" She stood, then strode in the direction the men had disappeared.

In the small, tidy kitchen, Dan reached for a platter while Beau held a cutting board in one hand and a butcher knife in the other.

"Pardon me," she said.

Both men looked her way.

"Can I talk to you for a minute, Beau?" She bit down on her bottom lip. "Alone."

Dan placed the platter down on the counter and reached for the open bottle of wine. "I'll see if the ladies need a refill."

Beau set down the cutting board and turned to face her. "Sure. Go ahead."

"I don't suppose you'd mind putting that knife down first."

Chapter Nine

Beau hefted the knife in his hand. Clearly Sofia had been annoyed with him, and he had countered it with a smile and his best Southern charm. But it hadn't worked. So he figured she'd come up with some kind of excuse and was going to tell him she was leaving.

"What's up?" he asked, placing the knife on the cutting board.

"I owe you an apology."

"No, I'm the one who owes you one. I shouldn't have kissed you. I was out of line. I know it upset you, and I didn't mean to do that. You were right to tell me to back off. I'm sorry."

"You didn't do anything wrong. I kissed you back. It's just that... Well, it was too much, too fast, too soon."

She'd dressed casually this evening—a tight-fitting pair of jeans and a white blouse, the top two buttons undone, revealing a simple yet delicate necklace. She shifted her weight to one hip, and the heart dangling from the silver chain shifted, too. She fingered it, then sighed. "Apology accepted. But I'm sorry, too. For my behavior earlier. I was rude."

Yes, she had been. He smiled and gave her a wink. "I hadn't noticed."

"Yeah, right."

She'd applied just enough makeup to make her brown eyes pop and to coat her lips in a pretty shade of pink. But it was her contrite expression he zeroed in on. It looked good on her. It made her seem human, caring. Approachable.

She released her necklace and dropped her hand to her side. "You have to understand. I've done everything on my own. I've worked hard to get to where I'm at, and I never..." She sucked in another breath, then slowly blew it out. "I have a rule. I never get involved with anyone I work with."

"Neither do I." Fishing off the company pier was a bad idea and only led to complications. "But this isn't the same thing. We don't work together, Sofia."

"We do at the high school. Temporarily, anyway. And once the course is finished, we'll be competitors again. So I shouldn't have let you kiss me. And worse, I shouldn't have kissed you back."

"I'm sorry it left you uneasy. And that you regret it."

"What I regret most is that I enjoyed it. Too much, I'm afraid. And it's made me…"

He filled in the blanks. "Uneasy. Uncomfortable. Unbalanced."

She nodded. "I'd say that pretty much covers it."

"I'll tell you what. Let's put that kiss behind us and pretend it didn't happen. Then, after our time at the high school is over, maybe we can go out to dinner and celebrate a job well done."

"That's not necessary. We might be teammates now, but after the project is over, we'll go back to being competitors."

She had a point. They were both intent upon winning. "Still, I owe you a celebratory dinner. You're a big reason the class is going over so well. Your organizational skills are amazing. And the kids like you, especially the girls because they can relate to you and they're impressed with your success."

At that, she smiled, and a light flush colored her cheeks. "The kids like you, too."

"I was hoping you'd say that. Because I never considered being a teacher, and I have to admit, it's been kind of cool. Not that I have any intention of changing careers."

"I wouldn't think so."

"Let's just say we're both on unsure footing. Neither of us is entirely certain what the future will bring. So we'll take it day by day. And no more kissing—at least until the Lone Star Best competition is over."

Her gaze held his, and something passed between them—an understanding of sorts. And mutual respect. He liked that.

"Are you still okay with water?" he asked. "Or do you want to change to wine or beer?"

She pondered the question for a beat, then said, "You know, I think I'm ready to switch to wine. But just a splash."

"You got it."

"We can talk more about this later—if we need to."

They'd definitely need to talk more. Moments after Sofia left the kitchen, Dan reentered. He didn't mention the private chat Sofia had requested, but the question hung in the air.

"It's all good," Beau said. At least, it seemed better.

Dan nodded. "Then let's get the food on the table and join the ladies."

"Good idea." Beau had no idea what the next few weeks would bring, but for the first time this evening, he'd begun to think that maybe, once the Lone Star Best competition was over and done, he and Sofia might have a future after all.

Maria had sat quietly in her seat, watching Dan linger in the living room while making small talk with Camila. He'd come from the kitchen with a wine bottle right after Sofia left and had offered to replenish their glasses, both of which still had plenty.

Minutes later, when Sofia reentered the room, Dan asked to be excused, then returned to the kitchen. Sofia didn't mention anything about the little chat that had gone on in private, but she didn't need to. She appeared to be at ease—and more herself.

Maria's chest filled with warmth—and a little ache, too. Sofia was such a bright, accomplished young woman. She was also beautiful and rarely wore a long face, like the one she'd worn ever since they arrived. Thank goodness she'd chased it away.

Maria had been looking forward to this evening from the very moment Beau had invited them. Sofia made no secret of the fact she'd found him attractive, at first anyway. Her big brown eyes had sparkled when she'd talked about running into him again at the dog park.

And why wouldn't Sofia be smitten with Beau? He was handsome, charming, successful. But before Maria put on her fairy godmother crown and moved full speed ahead with her matchmaking plans, she'd wanted to see where he lived and how he carried himself in familiar surroundings.

And she had to admit, so far this evening, she was impressed.

Many years ago, Carlos had impressed Maria, too. Oh, that man had been handsome. And charming. So she knew what those sparkles and the fire in Sofia's eyes meant.

The front door swung open, and a tall young man entered, his close-cropped, light brown curls damp from the rain. His casual clothing—sports attire—was every bit as stylish as Beau's.

Sofia gave him a careful once-over, although Maria didn't read any feminine interest in her eyes. No, it was more like curiosity. And she was making an assessment. Maria made one, too. Assuming he was Beau's brother, the Fortunes of New Orleans appeared to be a very handsome bunch.

"Hey, everyone. I'm Beau's brother Draper. I hope he's being a good host."

As if on cue, Beau entered the room, carrying a glass of wine, and offered it to Sofia, who took it.

Another good sign, Maria decided.

"Draper," Beau said, "I'd like you to meet the De Leons. Maria and Camila…" He opened his palm to the sofa first, then to the easy chair. "And Sofia."

"It's nice to meet you," Draper said. His gaze turned to Sofia. "I've heard a lot about you. I hope you're making my brother earn his keep at the high school."

"You better believe it." Sofia and Beau exchanged grins.

Yes, Maria thought. They were a good pair, even if they hadn't quite figured it out yet.

"If you'll excuse me," Draper said. "I'm going to change into some dry clothes."

Beau said something in a low tone to Sofia, and she laughed.

What a relief. In spite of the rain and the awkward beginning, things were going much better now.

Dan entered the room with a bottle of red wine. He approached Camila first. "Are you ready for the refill now?"

She flushed a pretty shade of pink, then nodded. "Please."

Dan appeared a little shy and the bottle trembled as he poured.

Maria nearly rubbed her hands together. So many potential romances. She hardly knew where to start!

For a while, Beau had worried that tonight's dinner party would be a complete failure. First, the rain had hit before he expected. And then a new waitress at Provisions had messed up his order. Then, to top it off, Sofia had arrived with a burr under her saddle.

But she'd agreed to put that kiss behind them, so things were better now.

As a result, they'd eaten their fill of grilled tri-tip, twice-baked potatoes, Caesar salad and the creamed corn he hadn't ordered. The conversation had flowed naturally, and as usual, Draper was the life of the party.

Truth be told, Dan and Sofia's mom had remained pretty quiet, but he'd spotted a few exchanged glances and timid smiles.

Even the dogs had quieted down, and now they were each enjoying a couple of rawhide chews Dan had given them.

"You sure are a good cook," Sofia's grandmother said.

"Coming from you, that's a real compliment." But Beau had never been one to accept false credit. "I'd like to say thank you, Maria, but Dan seasoned and grilled the meat. My only job was picking up the side dishes at Provisions. I'm afraid my sister Belle is the cook in our family."

"That reminds me," Draper said. "Belle called me while I was at the club with Ray Jennings. She and Jack would like to have us over for dinner at his house next week. She's making jambalaya."

"I'll be there," Beau said. "I'd never turn down

Grandma's jambalaya recipe." Beau turned to his guests and explained. "Jack Radcliffe runs the Pets2Vets program. He also works for Fortune Brothers Construction and rents a ranch house from Callum Fortune, his boss. Belle helped with the design/décor of the place, and now she and Jack are dating."

"I've been out to Jack's place," Dan said, "and I met his dog, Sarge. Jack's the one who talked me into adopting M.P."

Beau shot a glance at the rambunctious pup, who was chewing away on the rawhide bone.

"Jack's doing a good thing," Dan added. "Matching up veterans, some of them wounded and struggling, with dogs needing a home."

"I don't even know the man," Camila said, "but I couldn't agree more. He's doing a wonderful thing for the dogs and veterans in our community."

"Don't leave out Beau and Sofia," Maria added. "Their efforts are helping the teenagers in town."

Beau glanced at Sofia. It appeared that way. They'd certainly joined forces at Rambling Rose High School. He just hoped their tenuous bond would last past the competition.

The conversation continued until after they enjoyed the cherry pie that had inadvertently replaced the cheesecake Beau had ordered.

"Well," Sofia said, as she pushed aside the dessert plate that had once held a sliver of pie, "it's been a lovely evening. Thank you for inviting us."

Camila nodded. "The food was delicious—no matter whose hands prepared it."

Maria readily agreed. "We're having a game night next Saturday at our place."

Both Sofia and Camila shot her a surprised look, one that said "We are? Since when?"

"I hope you'll all attend. It'll be lots of fun."

"I'm free," Dan said.

It did sound like fun. And Beau didn't have any plans. "Sure. Why not?"

Not to be undone, Maria looked at Draper. "I hope you can make it, too. You're free to bring a guest, if you want."

"I'm afraid I'll be tied up. But thanks for asking. Maybe next time."

Beau suspected Ines, his latest date, would be back in town. Not that she and Draper had any kind of commitment. Draper didn't make them, although he was always upfront about that with the women he dated.

As the ladies stood, they reiterated their thanks. Sofia snapped a leash on Pepe, who still had the chew in his mouth.

"Let me and M.P. walk you out," Dan said.

He called his dog. They exchanged good-byes at the door, then Dan followed the ladies into the stormy night.

After Beau closed the door, he turned to Draper, whose grin stretched across his face. "You've got a good eye, bro. Let me know if you decide she's not your type."

"She's not *your* type."

Draper gave Beau's shoulder a playful punch. "I'm open to all types." It was a playful, brotherly tease, and no offense was taken. "I can see you like her, Beau. Good luck. I hope it works out for you."

"Thanks. I hope so, too."

The truth of the matter was, Sofia might have come from a different background than his, but she'd succeeded on her own. She was bright, determined and classy. So much so, that she might, in her own way, even have the Fortunes outclassed.

Chapter Ten

On Tuesday, moments before the bell rang, Beau helped Sofia set up the lesson plan. She looked more relaxed today in slacks with a V-neck knit top, and after the dinner the other night, their conversation had become more cooperative than combative.

The kids began taking their seats. Jamal Robertson, a tall, lanky pitcher on the RRHS baseball team, walked in just under the wire, with a swagger only a teen could pull off.

"Hey, Mr. Fortune," he said. "You guys told us that you weren't a couple, but you sure looked like one when you were dancing Saturday night."

The other students nodded, giggled and murmured in the affirmative.

Beau knew what they were thinking and why. He and Sofia definitely had chemistry. And that evening at the high school dance, they'd slipped into each other's arms as if they'd been together for years.

"Dancing was just part of the evening entertainment," Sofia said, her cheeks glowing pink. "The committee asked us to take part, and we were just being good sports."

Kelly Marshall, who'd been in charge of the dance committee, tucked a strand of long, blond hair behind her ear. "Thanks for chaperoning." She dropped her backpack on a desk in the second row. "We liked having a couple of young chaperones for a change."

"You're welcome. We had fun." Beau shot a "didn't we?" glance at Sofia, who smiled and nodded in agreement.

The air ventilation system's fan kicked on, blowing the scent of Sofia's perfume his way, sparking off the memory of holding her close, swaying to the beat of a sexy slow song, followed by thoughts of the heated kiss they'd shared.

Beau sobered. The "fun" had come to a dead stop once Sofia'd had second thoughts.

Fortunately, the bell rang, providing him with

a loud wake-up call and allowing him to slip into instructor mode.

"Listen up," he said. "We only have one class left after today, and we have a lot to cover. So let's get started."

Jose, one of the kids who always chose a desk in the front row, let out a sigh. "For a guy who wasn't looking forward to taking the class, I gotta admit, it's been pretty cool. I've learned a lot. And I'm sorry it's ending."

Beau had hoped the kids would feel that way. Before he could respond, Sofia stepped forward. "I think I can speak for Mr. Fortune when I tell you that we're sorry, too." This time she turned to him, and he nodded his agreement.

"All right, then. If you'll pass your homework to the person in front of you, I'll collect it."

Sofia made her way to the teacher's desk, where she'd placed the handouts. "Jose, will you please pass these around for us?"

The kids quieted down while Sofia collected the homework from those sitting at the desks in the front of the room.

Beau opened the discussion on income taxes and filing returns. Most people dreaded tax season and found it stressful, but the kids seemed to really get into it, especially since they'd been given two imaginary scenarios, complete with W-2 forms, a list of income and deductions and mock 1040 forms.

After the kids filed out of the room, Kelly took Sofia aside to talk privately.

Beau wished that, after they were finished chatting, he could take Sofia aside, too. But he knew better than to mix business with pleasure, especially when she was determined not to. And he damn sure wouldn't mention that kiss again. Ancient history.

As he slipped the homework into his briefcase, he couldn't help overhearing Kelly and Sofia's conversation.

"Ms. De Leon," Kelly said, "I have two questions. First of all, one of my friends wasn't able to take this class because she leaves before three to babysit her little brothers. She was wondering if you were going to offer it again in the fall."

"I'd like that very much, but I'd have to discuss that with Mr. Fortune as well as the principal." She looked at Beau as if wanting backup. But a lot could happen before September, so he gave a slight shrug.

Sofia returned her attention to Kelly. "What's the second question?"

"My sister is studying accounting at the University of Texas. She's in Austin now, but she's coming home for the summer and needs to find an internship. Is there any chance she could talk to you? I mean, you don't have to pay her or anything." Kelly cut a glance at Beau. "She wouldn't mind interning with you, either. It's just that my sister told me there's not a lot of women in her business courses, and I thought Ms. De Leon could give her some advice about competing in a male-dominated world."

Sofia smiled. "Tell her to email me—and put RRHS in the subject line."

Happy with her answer, Kelly thanked her, then left the classroom.

Beau had been tempted to tell Kelly that he would have been supportive of her sister, too. But he took the backseat. He hated to admit it, but Sofia would probably have more to offer her in that regard.

Sofia grabbed her briefcase, as well as the purse she'd stashed in the teacher's desk drawer.

"I'll walk you to your car," Beau said.

If she had any objections or concerns, she didn't let on. So they locked the classroom and left the building.

Once they reached the parking lot, he was tempted to ask if she had time for a cup of coffee, a glass of wine or...hell, he'd even be up for a milkshake, which might sound too juvenile for either one of them.

Instead, he said, "I'll see you on Thursday. And again on Saturday. That is, if game night is still on."

Her steps slowed, and she turned to him. A slight grin formed. "My mom told me it is."

"Will you be there?" he asked.

At that, she laughed. "I think my grandmother would shoot me if I didn't show up."

He hoped she'd say that. He wouldn't look forward to sitting around playing gin rummy or Monopoly with her mom and grandmother, although Dan said he was going. But that's because he seemed to be crushing on Camila, and it appeared to be mutual.

"I'll see you there." Sofia tossed him a pretty smile. Then she got into her car and pulled out of the parking lot.

Beau did the same. After calling Draper at the office and learning that he had it all under control, he headed home.

He'd just turned into his neighborhood when he spotted Dan walking M.P. down the street. So he pulled over to the side of the road and rolled down the passenger window. "Hey! Where are you two going? The dog park?"

Dan nodded. "I thought I'd let M.P. get some energy out."

"Good idea."

"I assume you've been at the high school. How's that class going?"

"Better than either Sofia or I expected. The kids seem to be enjoying it. And the principal and the other faculty members are pleased. Even some of the parents have commented that their kids seem to be a lot more frugal and future-minded."

"That's great. Wish I would have had a class like that before I joined the Army. I wouldn't have screwed up my credit and I would've been able to buy a house a lot sooner than I did."

"You were just a kid back then," Beau said. "At least, you got things turned around."

"Yeah. And thanks for talking to me about investing. After taking your advice, my 401K is looking a lot better, too."

"Hey, that's what friends are for."

"I know that class was part of the Lone Star Best competition, but it's been so successful. Would you consider offering it again?"

"Funny you should ask that. In fact, one of the kids brought it up today. The thought has definitely crossed my mind, too, but I'm not going to mention anything to Sofia. I'd rather the idea be hers."

"Big of you. I mean, smart." Dan nodded sagely. "How much longer does that class run?"

"It's over on Thursday."

"So that's the end of the first round of competition. Have you heard anything about what you'll have to do next?"

"Not a peep. I guess they'll call or email sometime next week. I sure wish they'd let us know sooner, although that might put a damper on our game night at the De Leons' house. Sofia's a gung-ho competitor."

"So are you." He pointed at Beau, and M.P. barked.

Beau grinned. "True. And I'll be persona non grata until the winners are announced."

"Then, I hope you don't hear anything from the committee until after game night."

Beau bet he did. His neighbor clearly had his eye on Sofia's mom.

"Can I catch a ride with you on Saturday?" Dan asked.

"Sure. I'll drive." Of course, Beau's answer might have been different if he'd thought there was any chance he and Sofia would make plans to do something afterward. But she'd been more than clear. They were teammates now. And then competitors. And even after the award winner was announced, the jury was still out on dating.

On Thursday, Sofia had been running behind schedule all day, which affected her arrival at the high school for their last class. She wasn't actually going to be late, though. She just liked to have plenty of time to gather her thoughts before the kids walked in.

Not that Beau's presence didn't make gathering her thoughts more difficult. After that kiss, being in the same room with him kept her a little off-balance, but so far, she'd managed to hold things together and present her lectures in a way that the kids could understand.

Just as she'd shut off the ignition, her cell phone rang. She almost let it roll over to voice mail, but when she spotted the number, she took the precious time to answer.

"Ms. De Leon?" the caller said. "This is Marcia McClain with the Lone Star Best. I'm calling to let you know that you'll be getting an email later this evening or tomorrow morning regarding the awards dinner that will be held at the Austin Grand Hotel next Friday night. I thought you might want to get it on your calendar."

"Thank you. I'll be there." She paused. That meant the final judging would need to take place before the awards dinner. "I do have a question for you, though. Will the email provide instructions for the second round?"

"The second round has already started. So keep an eye on your inbox. If you don't receive them by tomorrow afternoon, check your spam. And if they're still not there, give me a call at this number."

"All right," she said. After ending the call, she braced herself for the upcoming challenge. But what had Ms. McClain meant when she'd said the second round had already begun? That didn't make sense. Hopefully, she'd have a better idea when she read that email. Maybe Beau knew something. She tapped her fingernails on the steering wheel. If he did, would he tell her?

She'd soon find out. She left her car in the parking lot and hurried through the library and to the classroom, where she found Beau writing on the whiteboard. Damn. He looked good. He'd dressed casually again, but he still looked polished. And sexy. A white polo shirt with short sleeves revealed his muscular arms. His broad shoulders led down to a trim waist, and those tailored black pants fit him perfectly. In spite of herself, she took a moment to study him with fresh eyes—and sexual appreciation.

He must have heard her footsteps—or her soft panting—because he turned around, black marker in hand. When his eyes met hers, a dimpled grin embellished his gorgeous face. "Hey."

"Sorry I'm late."

"You're not. The bell hasn't rung. And I'm early."

"Have you heard from anyone on the Lone Star Best committee?" she asked with an annoying hitch in her voice.

"Yes. Did you?"

She nodded and cleared her throat. "They invited me to the awards ceremony next Friday. And they said we'd get an email tonight."

"That's what the woman told me, too. So, after today, I guess our teamwork is over."

Oddly enough, she wasn't quite ready for that. But that's how this game was to be played. And won.

"Did she give you any hints about the second round?" Sofia asked. "She told me that's it's already started."

"I didn't ask. I assumed that she meant it would start tonight, after the workday is over, and that we'd get the details in the email."

Sofia nodded. "You're probably right." Yet it still seemed a little confusing. Why hadn't they explained more before this?

Nevertheless, as the first bell rang and the kids began to arrive, she did her best to shake off her misgivings.

Before she knew it, the class had ended, and the kids stood and gave them a standing ovation. Several of them mentioned their disappointment, which pleased her. She—okay, Beau, too—had put a lot of time and effort into presenting the world of finance to the students.

"Before you go, I have something for you." Sofia reached into her briefcase, pulled out the ten-dollar gift certificates she'd asked her assistant to purchase and place in official, letterhead envelopes. Once in hand, she passed them out. "You guys didn't have to take this class, so this is to thank you from De Leon Financial Consulting for participating."

At that, Billy Mitchell piped up. "I didn't have much choice. I had to take it. The vice-principal said he'd knock off my detention hours if I took part. So now I'm free as a bird."

Several kids laughed.

Kelly glanced at the card and smiled. "Awesome. I love Kirby's Perks."

"You love their sweet coffee milkshakes with whipped cream on top," her friend Maya Rainwater said, sticking out her tongue. "And now you can feed your addiction."

"So what?" Kelly grinned from ear to ear. "Thanks, Ms. De Leon. And thanks to both of you. This was the best class I've had all year."

"Be sure to write that in your class review," Sofia said. "The principal and the school board would like to know your thoughts about what you learned and what we might have done differently."

"You got it."

Sofia hoped most, if not all, of the students would rave about the class. She wasn't sure how the Lone Star Best would score their project— either jointly or individually. But whenever she took on a project, she gave it her all. And she liked knowing her efforts were appreciated.

After the kids left the classroom, Beau closed the distance between them and lowered his voice.

"Nice touch, Sofia. Gift cards? That certainly shows your competitive side."

Maybe she should have said they were from both companies, but it had been a last-minute decision. Besides, it didn't hurt for him to know they were competitors again.

"Whatever do you mean?" She tried to keep her tone light and innocent. "You could have done something similar."

"You want the kids to like you better than they like me."

That was hard to deny, since it was true. They were great kids. And she couldn't refute having the heart of a competitor, especially when she was up against Beau. But winning anyone's affection hadn't been her motive when she sent her assistant to Kirby's Perks.

She crossed her arms. "The gift cards weren't a bribe. They were a thank-you for a job well done. Hard work should be rewarded. Besides, you're just sorry you didn't think of it."

A soft chuff turned into a smile, and he winked. "Maybe."

She unfolded her arms. "Come on, Beau. I'll walk *you* to your car."

"All right." He extended his arm in an after-you fashion. "Thanks for bringing those gift certificates. It was a nice gesture."

That's what she thought. But if truth be told,

Kirby's Perks' gift cards or not, she wouldn't mind if the kids liked her best. She wanted to win, and she wasn't ashamed of her ambition—nor would she apologize for it.

After Beau left the high school, he drove to the office. Once inside the spacious lobby of Fortune Investments, he walked to the reception desk, where a bouquet of fresh flowers, delivered by Petunia's Posies each Monday, greeted each visitor.

Gretchen Williams, the newly hired receptionist, looked up from her work and smiled. "Good afternoon, Mr. Fortune."

He'd asked her to call him Beau twice, but apparently, she didn't feel comfortable doing so. He offered her a smile. "How's it going, Gretchen?"

"Great. The mail was late, so I'm sorting it now. I'll bring it in momentarily."

"Thanks." Beau continued through the doorway and into the main office, where Draper stood next to the mahogany table that held the Remington sculpture they had on display. The Bronco Buster wasn't an original, which would have cost a mint, but it was an official reproduction the brothers had purchased early this year. It seemed appropriate for a Texas office and added to the Western-themed decor.

"I'm back," Beau said.

Draper, who wore a designer suit, his customary business attire, turned and shot him a grin. "It's good to see you're still in one piece. Teenagers can be brutal."

"Fortunately, the teens Sofia and I have been working with are great kids." He didn't see any point in mentioning that he was going to miss them or the assignment. "How'd things go here?"

"It's been fairly quiet all afternoon," Draper said.

Beau scanned the lobby. "Where's Belle?"

"She had to run an errand and said she'd be back 'in a few.'" Draper glanced at the clock. "She should be here any time."

"Good to know. I had a couple of questions I wanted to ask her about the Flannigan account. I try to stay on top of my clients, but I'm afraid I've been a little distracted by that class."

"I'd think Sofia might be your biggest distraction." Draper chuckled. "How many more classes do you have to teach?"

"Today was the last one." Beau told his brother about the phone call he'd received from the Lone Star Best committee and the awards dinner in Austin. "I hope you can make it next Friday night."

"I'll have to reschedule something, but I'll be there."

"Good. I'm glad."

"Thanks again for taking that high school project on for us," Draper said. "I didn't mean to dump it on you."

"I know. And you're welcome." Beau had been a little annoyed at first, but as it turned out, his brother had inadvertently done him a big favor. The kids had been awesome, and he'd actually enjoyed working with Sofia.

The lobby door swung open, and Belle, dressed in her usual business chic style—designer black pants and jacket, white silk camisole and a colorful scarf that probably cost more than the rest of the ensemble—swept into the room. When she spotted Draper and Beau, her eyes lit up, but she didn't smile. Instead, she picked up her pace and crossed the room, her high heels clicking upon the tile floor.

"I was hoping to catch you both together," she said. "Joanna Singleton called and wanted to cash out half of her account and invest elsewhere."

Beau frowned. "Why? She seemed happy with her investments the last time I talked to her."

Belle arched her brow. "Apparently, she has a teenage relative—a great niece or something— who took a finance class at Rambling Rose High. And the girl raved about one of her instructors."

"No kidding?" Beau folded his arms across his chest. "She's moving her account to De Leon Financial Consulting?"

"Just half of it," Belle said. "I told her we'd get

the paperwork in order, but I suggested she talk to you first."

Beau blew out a sigh. The Singleton account wasn't his largest, but it was sizable. "I guess Sofia really impressed her niece."

Draper placed a hand on Beau's back. "Hopefully you won't lose any other accounts to a business rival."

Damn. Beau hadn't seen that coming. Well, there wasn't much he could do about it, although he would give Joanna a call.

"Listen," Belle said. "I'd like to cut out early—if you guys don't mind. Jack and I have dinner plans, and I'd like to get out of these heels and into something more comfy."

"Have a nice evening," Beau told his sister.

She smiled. "Oh, I will."

Beau grimaced. "Please. You're still my baby sister. I don't want to hear about what goes on in your bedroom." He ducked as she threw a pen at him.

"Get your brain out of the gutter, bro," she said. "We're going over some ideas for my boutique over dinner."

"Sounds like a good night, sis. Now that you're here," Draper said, "I'm going to call it a day, too, Beau. I'll see you at the house."

"What? No date tonight? Is Ines still out of town?"

"Yes, but she and I don't have any kind of commitment, which suits us both. So I could go out if I wanted to. But I've got an early tee time at the country club out by Rambling Rose Estates tomorrow."

"Did you join?"

"Not yet. I thought I'd take you out there first. I wouldn't join without your okay."

"We can talk more about it later," Beau said. "There's no need to rush into anything."

"I agree." Draper started toward his office, then stopped. "By the way, are you free Saturday evening? It's prime rib night at the club, and the head chef is pretty good. We've been invited to sit at the owner's table."

That was a big deal. If the owner took him and Draper under his wing, they'd have entry to the Who's Who of Rambling Rose. But the thought of Sofia sitting across the table from him for an entire evening, even if it was only as bridge partners, made the club seem like just another stuffy business meeting with food.

"Maybe another time," Beau said. "I've got plans." As the words rolled off his tongue, a slow smile began to stretch across his face.

Who would've ever guessed that Beau Fortune would pass up a steak dinner with some of the Rambling Rose elite for a night of Parcheesi, dominoes, bingo or whatever else the De Leon women had in mind? But he had. And damned if he wasn't looking forward to it.

Chapter Eleven

There was something cozy about the elder De Leons' dining room that reminded Beau of an old 1960s rom-com movie. Maybe it was the floral paintings on the wall. Or the way the five of them sat in chairs around an antique table draped with a cream-colored tablecloth that had been freshly laundered—and no doubt hand pressed.

More likely, though, it was because Beau couldn't take his eyes off Sofia, who wore her hair in a long braid, revealing a pair of diamond studs.

"Yahtzee!" Camila called out, clapping her hands. "I won again!"

"That's three in a row," Dan said. "You're hot to-night. You'd better buy a couple of lottery tickets."

Camila smiled. "I'm not usually very lucky. I'm sure those tickets will be a waste of time—and money." She turned to her daughter. "What is it you always say?"

Sofia laughed. "The lottery is a tax on people who aren't good at math."

Beau sat back in his chair and grinned. "You've got that right. But it's fun to gamble once in a while, and a single ticket only costs a dollar."

In fact, it was fun to kick back and be a kid sometimes, something he rarely did anymore. He might be a grown man now and no longer a boy living in NOLA, but he'd had a blast tonight playing kids' games, which left him pleasantly surprised.

"I'll make some coffee and bring out a plate of sweets," Maria said.

When Camila and Sofia got to their feet, apparently intending to help, the older woman waved them off. "Oh no, you don't! You two stay here and visit with our guests."

Was Maria just trying to be a good hostess? Or was she hoping to see a match or two between the couples?

It certainly seemed like she had an alternative motive. Not that it bothered him. Hell, not in the least. But she'd undoubtedly be more successful in pairing up Dan and Camila. Those two had been sharing smiles all night.

On the other hand, Sofia was pleasant enough—and she'd laughed along with everyone else at times—but he'd sensed that she was holding back, that she was always ready to put up a strong defense.

He suspected that she was maintaining an emotional distance from him and gearing up for more competition.

Oddly enough, the email he'd received from the committee didn't explain much. The second round had somehow been completed, although he'd be darned if he knew what the parameters were or how the scores had been tabulated. They'd find out soon enough, though. Maybe not knowing where either of them stood had something to do with Sofia's quiet demeanor. But Beau wouldn't bring it up. Why risk ruining the evening?

"Camila." Dan cleared his throat and managed a shy smile. "I've had a great time this evening. I don't suppose you'd consider going to dinner with me sometime."

Sofia's mom blinked twice, as if the question had taken her aback, and adjusted her red reading glasses. Then she fingered the amber gem that dangled from the delicate gold chain around her neck.

Yep. She was definitely shaken. And Beau felt a bit sorry for his neighbor.

Camila glanced first at her daughter, then back

to Dan. "I—I haven't gone out to dinner in years. Maria is such a good cook. Goodness, I'm not sure I remember how to read a menu."

"It's like riding a bike," Dan said. "You never forget."

Camila grinned, and her cheeks flushed.

Sofia offered her an understanding smile. "You need to get out more often, Mama."

Camila nodded and dropped her hand, releasing her necklace, and turned to Dan. "All right, then."

Dan took a deep breath, as if he was about to carefully step out on a limb. Then he slowly let it out. "Are you free next Friday evening?"

That was the night of the Lone Star Best Awards dinner. Had Sofia invited Camila to attend as her guest? Maybe, because her mom didn't answer right away.

Finally, she said, "I don't have any plans."

Dan's cautious expression morphed into a smile. "Great. I'll pick you up at six." He shot a glance at Beau, then at Sofia. "Would you two like to join us?"

The poor guy was looking for backup, and under other circumstances, Beau would help him out. But there was no way Sofia would agree to a double date, even if they were both free. She'd made it clear that she wouldn't consider any kind of relationship with him, other than professional, until after the competition ended. And he'd just have to be satisfied with waiting to see how she felt then.

Although here they were together at game night, acting pretty damned friendly. Mixed signals? He gazed across the table into her expressive brown eyes, framed with thick dark lashes. He yearned to hold her in his arms and kiss her again.

Man, what're you thinking? Cut. It. Out.

Sofia tore her gaze away from his. "Beau and I are both busy on Friday. That's the night of the Lone Star Best dinner."

"She's right. We're both going to be in Austin." An idea struck, one that seemed logical and convenient, something Beau hadn't considered until now. "Sofia, why don't we ride together?"

Her lips parted, and her shoulders stiffened.

"As team partners," Beau added. "Besides, Austin is a good hour away."

Sofia slowly shook her head. "I think it's best if we take separate cars."

Beau knew what she was thinking. That way, no one would assume they were dating—especially Beau.

"It'll be awkward for you on the return trip," she added, "because I'm going to win."

"No problem." Beau winked. "But don't be too sure about winning."

She tossed him a skeptical grin.

"And as for going separately, don't forget that

they assigned seating at the luncheon. So, it seems likely that we'll be sitting at the same table."

"You might be right."

"If it makes you feel better," he added, "my brother is going, too."

"Good. But I'm still driving myself."

"Look," Beau said. "Someone is going to win, and someone is going to lose. It won't bother me who ends up with the trophy. Unless, of course, you think you can't handle it when you lose?"

"Don't be ridiculous."

After a couple of beats, she bit down on her bottom lip. Stewing about his suggestion, he supposed.

Then his thoughts came back to haunt him. *Take it easy. You're trying too hard, buddy.*

Too late to backpedal. He'd just lobbed the ball over the net. And it was in her court now.

Beau had a point. The contest might be out of Sofia's hands, although that didn't mean she'd agree to ride with him to the dinner. On the upside, his brother's presence would be helpful. That way, she and Beau wouldn't appear to be a twosome. It certainly hadn't taken very long for the kids at the high school to make that assumption.

"Just to be clear," she said. "I appreciate your offer to carpool, but I'm going to Austin early. There's a boutique I want to visit before the event."

Beau nodded. "Okay, but if you change your mind…"

"I won't." She softened her quick response with a smile. "And, by the way, I'm glad Draper is going with you. Fortune Investments should be represented by the two of you."

With both brothers seated at the table, it would be easier for Sofia to focus on something other than that tempting, blood-stirring attraction she felt whenever she and Beau were together. An attraction she'd hoped would pass in time. Instead, it had only grown stronger. And even more so tonight.

Attending Abuelita's game night had been a bad idea. Sofia should have faked a headache and stayed home.

She glanced across the table. Beau had begun to gather up the dice, score sheets and pencils.

Mama got to her feet. "I'll take those."

Beau handed them to her and offered her a charming smile.

Maybe if things were different, Sofia wouldn't be so dead set on fighting her attraction. But right now, with so much at stake, she considered any remotely romantic feelings for him a weakness. And if there was anything Sofia didn't need, especially before a competition, was a chink in her armor.

Don't be too sure about winning, Beau had said.

She chuffed inwardly. Beau was so sure of himself. But that didn't surprise her. They both knew his last name might give him an edge over her. She would just have to hope that the final judges would remain impartial.

Abuelita returned carrying a tray with coffee and a plate filled with the goodies she'd baked earlier—sour cream jumbos, Mexican sweet bread and brownies.

Beau immediately complimented her. "Maria, that bread looks delicious. It reminds me of the semester I spent in Guadalajara."

Abuelita beamed. "It's my mother's recipe. I think you'll like it."

Mama returned to the table and helped Abuelita pass around the cups of the freshly made brew. Sofia opted to drink hers black. The evening had been sweet enough already.

It had been nice to see Dan take an interest in Mama—and vice versa. He seemed to be a good man. Upright, honest, just. He'd also adopted a rescue dog, which suggested he had a kind heart.

She took a sip of the black coffee, which was still hot. She softened her stance a bit and poured in a splash of cream to cool it down. Oh, what the heck. She added a bit of sugar, too.

The others at the table laughed at something Abuelita had said, but Sofia had been so caught up in her thoughts that it had slipped by her. Still, she smiled as if she'd been engaged in the conversation.

Actually, there'd been plenty of smiles, laughs and chuckles this evening. She hated to admit it, but Beau had a nice sense of humor. She'd picked up on it before, but she'd disregarded it for some reason.

She stole another glance across the table. He had a nice set of arms on him, too—not to mention those long, denim-clad legs.

On the outside, he appeared to be one of the good guys. She probably ought to let down her guard and take a chance on dating him. But not until after the competition ended.

And maybe not even then. Something told her the two of them would always be competitors. It was part of their DNA.

And there was no getting around it.

It had been a long and busy week, which was helpful. Sofia had been able to keep her mind on her work and avoid thinking too much about the Lone Star Best Awards ceremony and the black-tie dinner.

On Friday afternoon, she left the office early to give herself plenty of time to get ready, which shouldn't be too difficult. She had a closet full of clothes, all organized from casual to formal—the colors grouped together. When she was a girl, there'd been very little money to purchase new dresses and outfits, which meant she'd had to rely on hand-me-downs from neighbors and friends. So once her career had taken off, she'd made sure that she had plenty to choose from.

Nevertheless, she'd found herself stewing over what to wear. She finally settled on a classic black dress, the newest of several others that hung in the closet. She also fussed with her hair and makeup longer than usual.

She told herself that it was important to look her best. There would be reporters and photographers present. But unfortunately, as much as she hated to admit it, Beau would be center stage with the media reps.

After applying a final layer of mascara, she hung a wrap over her shoulders and took one last look in the mirror. "That's as good as it gets." Then she drove to Austin with a flock of butterflies in her stomach.

The Lone Star Best folks had advised her to arrive early, so she'd allowed for plenty of time to get there. Still, thanks to heavier than usual traffic on Friday afternoon, she had to skip the visit to the boutique and got to the hotel a bit later than she'd hoped. After leaving her car with the valet, she entered the hotel and made her way to the ballroom. A rather dapper-looking gentleman in his sixties sat at the reception desk. "Good evening."

"I'm Sofia De Leon," she said. "One of the nominees."

He smiled. "I recognize your name. We have
five reserved tables for the VIPs. You'll be at table
three. Congratulations on the nomination. And
good luck."

"Thank you." She turned away from the table, but
before she could take a step, she spotted Beau and
his brother approach wearing tuxedos she doubted
they'd had to rent. Black-tie events were probably
commonplace for anyone in the Fortune family.

Both men wore them well, but it was Beau
who'd caught her eye and commanded her undi-
vided attention as he walked toward her.

Damn.

"You look lovely tonight, Sofia. And you're not
even wearing red." He smiled at the reference to
the song lyrics they'd danced to, and admiration lit
his eyes. She couldn't help feeling a wee bit giddy
at the compliment—and the shared memory.

But double damn. He was throwing her off her
game again.

Apparently, Draper had checked in for both
of them, because when he walked up and looked
down at her card, he said, "We're also sitting at
table three."

Beau motioned toward the doorway. "Shall
we?"

Sofia led the way to their seats, where they

joined four other nominees—a man and woman representing the arts and two men involved in the science industry.

The interesting conversations that took place were thought-provoking as well as impressive. But Sofia had a hard time keeping focused. Her thoughts and her eyes kept flitting to Beau, who was sitting beside her. At least, until the MC stepped to the podium.

"Excuse me," the man said. "My name is John Contreras. On behalf of the Lone Star Best committee, I'd like to welcome you to our tenth annual awards ceremony. We have some surprises for you this evening, but first, let's eat."

The waitstaff moved in to serve the first course, Caesar salad, followed later by the entrée. The presentation was lovely, and it probably tasted as good as it looked, but Sofia was so excited and nervous that she only took a couple bites of the salmon filet, rice pilaf and asparagus with hollandaise sauce.

Finally, the MC returned to the podium and began the ceremony. "As you know, the first round of our competition had to do with teamwork. Each of our nominees was assigned a project that would benefit various communities. But this year, we decided to run the second round differently than we'd done in the past. Instead of separating the original pair and assigning a new project, we sent out score sheets to all the individuals and the various entities that were on the receiving end of their time and efforts."

Murmurs filled the room. Sofia turned to Beau, her brow furrowed. "Did they ask the kids to score us?"

He appeared to be as surprised as she was. "That's what it sounds like. But maybe the school administration scored us based upon those student reviews."

"I'd assumed we were given a team review. But there must have been separate score sheets."

"Apparently."

As the MC began to speak, the ballroom grew silent. "Imagine our surprise when we learned that the highest scores were given to the nominees representing the same industry. And not only that, we had a tie!"

A flutter of nervousness rolled through Sofia's stomach. She scanned the faces of the others at her table. They all appeared intrigued. And hopeful.

"Since there was a tie," the MC said, "the committee went into an executive session last night to choose a winner. We did this by reading and digesting the answers to the essay question. That said, it's my pleasure to present this year's Lone Star Best Award to Beau and Draper Fortune of Fortune Investments."

Applause filled the ballroom, but it took a cou-

ple of beats for Sofia to swallow her disappointment, feign a smile and clap her hands.

"Congrats, boys," Sofia said.

Beau squeezed her shoulder as he stood.
"Thanks. But you were robbed."

"No, you deserved it." But seriously? There was
no way anyone could convince Sofia that the Fortune name hadn't given Beau and Draper—Texas
newcomers, for goodness' sake!—the edge. But
wasn't that the way the system worked?

As the brothers went to the dais to accept their
award, Sofia did her best to control her expression. People might think she was jealous, but she
wasn't. She felt cheated, though, since the competition hadn't really been fair.

She always wanted to win. So much so, that she
couldn't seem to focus on the Fortune brothers'
acceptance speech.

"Coffee?" a waiter asked her. "Or would you
rather wait for the champagne to be served?"

Celebrate a win for Fortune Investments? She'd
need a double shot of tequila just to fake it. And
even then, she wouldn't dance on the table.

She pointed at her cup, and the waiter poured
the coffee. Her thoughts rolled back to Thursday
afternoon, when she'd said good-bye to the class
and passed out the Kirby's Perks' gift certificates.

Nice touch, Beau had said. *But it shows your*

competitive side. You want the kids to like you bet-
ter than they like me.

Apparently, they didn't. The kids had clearly
chosen him over her. Had they been swayed by
his last name, too?

After all her hard work? Beau might have come
up with the initial idea, but she'd created the game
cards and put a lot of thought into all the scenarios
the kids had been given.

As Beau and Draper returned to the table with
their star-shaped crystal plaque, Sofia managed
to conjure a smile.

"There's another first this year," the MC said,
and the ballroom grew quiet. "After receiving the
reviews and going over them carefully, the Lone
Star Best committee decided to create a new award
this year. We're calling it The Lone Star Visionary
Award. We're proud to present it to an amazing
company led by a very bright CEO with vision,
one who has made a unique contribution to the
financial health of women and who's served as a
wonderful role model to the community of Rambling Rose. It's my honor and pleasure to present
this award tonight to Sofia De Leon and De Leon
Financial Consulting."

The announcement stunned her, and it took a
moment for her to comprehend what was happening. The kids, the high school staff and even the

committee had realized they had a real tie on their hands.

"Congratulations," Beau said, leaning forward and giving her a light kiss on the cheek. "Go on. Get up there."

Sofia got to her feet and made her way to the dais, accepting the award with grace and appreciation. A competition, she supposed, didn't get any better than this.

Once she held her own crystal trophy, a bit different yet similar in size to Beau's, she stepped in front of the microphone and tried her best to give the speech she'd rehearsed but no longer could remember.

"Thank you. This is a lovely surprise. I'm not usually speechless, but…" She cleared her throat. "I'd like to start by thanking my mother and grandmother, who sacrificed to put me through college. They taught me the meaning of hard work and determination, and it led me to create De Leon Financial Consulting, a firm that prides itself on teaching investment strategies to women while helping them build their portfolios. I'd also like to thank Rambling Rose High School for allowing Mr. Fortune and I to present a financial class geared to teenagers.

"I think I can speak for Mr. Fortune when I say the kids were amazing and an absolute joy to work with." She paused and her gaze sought Beau, who was looking at her with pride. "I'd be remiss if I didn't acknowledge Beau Fortune. We might be competitors, but you were a great teammate. It was a pleasure working with you."

The applause continued until she reached her table. When she took her seat, she pushed her coffee cup aside and placed the award on the table, a few inches from Beau's.

"How about that?" Beau offered her a flute of champagne, and she took it. "We're both in the winner's circle."

After tapping her crystal glass against his and then his brother's, she took a sip of the refreshing bubbly.

"I knew you were initially disappointed," Beau said. "But it worked out great in the end."

She hated to admit to any disappointment, but that would have been a lie. And he never would have believed her anyway. "Yes, a little. And you're right. I actually like being considered a—" She lifted her hands and made quotation marks in the air "— 'a visionary and a role model, especially to women.'"

"I couldn't agree more," Beau said.

"Hold that thought." Sofia dug her phone out of her purse. "Give me a minute. I promised to text my mom and grandmother as soon as I had any news—good or bad. And this is definitely good."

After she sent off the text, she returned her cell phone to her purse.

Beau lifted his flute. "Here's to the best teammate I've ever had—in business or sports."

"I'll drink to that." Sofia raised her glass and tapped it against his again. And when Draper lifted his, too, they toasted their success.

Sofia took another sip. Hmm. Had she ever tasted champagne this good?

Before she knew it, they'd each finished the first glass.

Draper poured them a second. "Good job, you two. I love being in the winner's circle."

The three of them chatted among themselves, and Sofia gave Draper a rundown of their school project. She also shared a few interesting moments they'd had with the kids. After pouring herself yet another glass she felt more open and talkative than she'd ever felt in a professional setting. She even told Draper about chaperoning the high school dance—something Beau had failed to tell him.

When she related the details of the featured dance, Draper turned to his brother and winked. "Don't tell me. It was a slow dance."

Beau nodded, and Draper laughed.

"What's so funny?" Sofia asked.

"Nothing. Really. We both thought we'd left our teenage years behind. And slow dancing in a gymnasium takes us both back to that time."

Draper might have laughed, but Beau hadn't. And neither did Sofia. There's no way that dance had reminded her of the old days. Because it was a grown man who'd held her in his arms. She and Beau had both shared a special moment on that dance floor. And that moment was even more intimate when he walked her to her car. Her cheeks warmed at the memory of that kiss that had left her breathless.

For that reason, she'd gathered her wits and put a stop to it, but for some reason, now that the competition was over, she was open to another kiss.

"Are you ready for more champagne?" Draper asked.

Sofia nodded, then she blinked. Uh-oh. She'd lost track of how many glasses she'd had. And she was feeling a bit woozy. She placed her hand over the top of her flute. "No, as good as it tastes, I'd better not. It's already gone right to my head."

"You feeling okay?" Beau placed a hand on her arm, warming her to the bone. "You didn't eat much."

True, she'd been too nervous to eat more than a few bites of her dinner. And she realized she was in no condition to drive home right now. She'd need to walk it off and drink some coffee.

"I'll tell you what," Beau said. "I'll drive you back in your car. Then I can take an Uber home."

"Are you sure? I don't want to put you out."

"Not to worry. I'd be happy to do it."

"In that case," Draper said, glancing at his watch, "I'll take off now. I've got an early tee time tomorrow and didn't get much sleep last night."

"Is Ines back in town?" Beau asked.

"No. I'm meeting Jillian at the golf course near Rambling Rose Estates, then we're going to her house for lunch and a swim."

Ines? Jillian? Draper didn't seem to have a shortage of dates. Sofia had heard through the grapevine that he was a player. But then again, he was both handsome and rich.

"Have fun, bro."

Sofia took a sip of her cold coffee.

"Wait," Beau called out to his brother. "You forgot—"

Sofia glanced up and scanned the ballroom, but Draper was already gone.

Beau shrugged. "Guess I'll be taking the trophy back with me."

With us, Sofia thought as she smiled. If truth be told, she was happy Beau had offered to drive her home—for more reasons than one.

Chapter Twelve

When the MC announced that Fortune Investments had won the Lone Star Best Award, Beau had been more than pleased, but he'd known winning would affect whatever chance he had of developing a meaningful relationship with Sofia. And not in a good way.

He hadn't been oblivious to her reaction to the announcement, either. Before he even got to his feet to accept the award, he'd noticed her expression. Both surprise and disappointment danced across her face, and he'd known there wasn't a damn thing he could do to make her feel better. So when the committee recognized her accomplishments in the workplace as well as the effort she'd put into the school project, he'd been both relieved and elated.

The way he saw it, it had been a very tight competition, and they both had a lot to celebrate. He wasn't surprised that she'd gotten a little tipsy after the champagne. And it didn't bother him a bit to drive her home.

Beau held his trophy in one hand and opened the passenger door of Sofia's Lexus with the other. "In you go."

"Thanks." As she climbed into the seat, her skirt slipped up to reveal her shapely thighs. She held her trophy against her chest and grinned at him. "Gotta keep this baby safe."

Warmth spread across his chest and rose up to his face. Damn, she was beautiful—whether she was a little tipsy or completely sober and challenging him head to head.

"Want me to hold yours, too?" she asked.

"You've got your hands full. I'll put it on the floor in the backseat."

Once they were on the road and headed back to Rambling Rose, Beau turned on the radio and scanned the channels until he found a classic rock station. The music set a romantic tone in the car, but when he glanced across the seat, he saw that it'd had a different effect on Sofia. It had lulled her to sleep.

With her prized trophy held in her arms and her pretty head pressed against the passenger-door window, her eyes closed and her lips parted, she looked sweet. Maybe even angelic. There was a vulnerability about her, although he'd never mention anything like that to her. Not when she prided herself on being a strong and competent business-woman. And more importantly, one that was successful and self-made.

She dozed most of the way home, waking only when he turned into her condominium complex.

"Oh." She straightened, adjusted the trophy in her lap, then rubbed her eyes. "We're already home."

Yep. Home.

"How are you feeling?" he asked.

"All right." She pointed to the right. "My garage is on the back side of my unit. Number 176."

"Got it."

As he turned the car, the headlights shined on a couple of neighbors walking a dog. But it wasn't just anyone. It was Maria, who held the end of Pepe's leash, with Camila strolling beside her.

Beau pulled to the side of the road and slowed to a stop as Sofia rolled down her window.

"Hey," Sofia said. "What are you two doing up so late? And why are you outside? It's chilly. And dark."

"We were just taking Pepe for a bedtime walk,"

Camila said. "Congratulations, you two. Wonderful news."

"Thanks," Beau called through the open window.

"Yes, thank you, Mama." Sofia shot Beau a smile. "We have a lot to celebrate."

"We couldn't be happier for you," Maria added. "Both of you!"

"I know that I asked you to keep Pepe overnight," Sofia said. "But I can take him with me now."

Maria waved her off. "We already told him he's staying with us. I don't want to confuse him. Or disappoint him."

Beau could scarcely keep a straight face. Surely Maria didn't believe the dog actually understood what they'd told him.

"Good night," Camila said. "Enjoy your success this evening. We'll see you tomorrow."

Sofia rolled up her window.

As the older De Leon women headed home, Beau was about to raise his window, too, when he heard the two women giggle. Their voices were hushed, and they spoke in Spanish, but he was able to pick up a few words. *Los novios.*

"Oh, those two," Sofia said, shaking her head.

A grin tugged at his lips. So they thought he and Sofia were lovers, huh? Maybe, with a little time and luck, they would be.

When they reached Sofia's garage, she pushed the button on the rearview mirror that had been programmed to open the door, and it rolled up.

"Would you like to come in and have a cup of coffee?" she asked.

He'd be delighted. "Sure." He parked in her garage.

It didn't surprise him to see it neatly organized, with rows of shelves lining the walls.

As Sofia went inside, he retrieved his trophy from the backseat. He wasn't going to lie. He was glad he'd won. And knowing that Sofia's accomplishments had been recognized only made his win sweeter.

Moments later, while Sofia prepared a pot of coffee, Beau scanned the clean white kitchen with a farmhouse-style sink, granite countertops and state of the art appliances. It suited her—light but warm. Modern and functional, yet top of the line.

He set his trophy on the counter, next to hers. Then he pulled her key fob from his pocket. "Is it okay if I leave this here?"

"Sure." She flipped the coffeemaker switch on, and it roared to life. "It'll be ready in a minute. Are you hungry?"

"No, I'm good." But he was hungry to kiss her again, not that he would.

"Why don't we sit in the living room while the coffee brews?"

He followed her out the doorway. She'd only taken a couple of steps when she stopped and her breath caught. "Why those sneaky women. They weren't just taking Pepe for a walk." She pointed to the coffee table, where apparently Maria and Camila had placed a silver bucket holding a bottle of champagne on ice, along with two flutes flanking a platter of chocolate-covered strawberries.

"I wondered what they were doing this late at night," Sofia said. "So what do you think? I don't want those strawberries to go to waste."

"They won't." Beau reached for the neck of the bottle. "Should we open it? Or do you want to have coffee and wait to celebrate until another day?"

"I've probably had enough champagne already, but we both have a lot to be happy about tonight. So we may as well open it. I'll get a dish towel for you to use while you pop the cork."

She kicked off her heels, and returned to the kitchen. While she was gone, he took a moment to check out her condo, which seemed to be a bigger floor plan than her mother's. She'd decorated her place in a style his sister Belle would call "farmhouse shabby chic." The walls were covered in shiplap, and the wide-plank floors were adorned with faded blue area rugs. The couches were off-white and looked as comfortable and fluffy as clouds.

Not bad, he thought. Straightforward neutral furnishings with a pop of blue here and there. It suited her, he decided. And the color scheme gave off a relaxing vibe.

Sofia returned with the dish towel. "Here you go."

He wrapped the cloth over the top of the bottle to prevent a spill, then popped the cork and poured them each a glass.

"Have a seat." She indicated the sofa. He complied, and she followed suit, sitting just close enough to reach out and touch him, yet allowing enough space to let him know she wasn't making a move on him.

Not that he'd mind if she did. It would make things easier that way. She was hard to read sometimes. He figured that was a defense mechanism she'd developed. And mastered.

She turned to face him, closing the distance a bit, and took a sip of champagne. "You know, once I learned your name, I didn't expect to like you. But I do."

"You sound surprised."

"Actually, I am." She ran the tip of her tongue across her top lip—not in a flirtatious manner, yet it had the same effect on him.

"Now that the competition is over," he said, "will you go out to dinner with me?"

"The Lone Star Best Award is over. But we're still business competitors."

"I don't see why. Your focus is on women."

"We have male clients, too." She reached for the plate of strawberries, picked up one and offered it to him.

"Thanks." He took a bite. Damn, it was juicy and sweet. Chocolaty, too. "Aren't you going to have one?"

"When I finish this." She lifted her flute, smiled and then took another sip. "I really like champagne. It tickles my nose."

She'd clearly lowered her guard, but he wasn't going to take advantage of it. Not when he suspected that the bubbly had also lowered her inhibitions. Still, he enjoyed seeing her smile.

"You have a nice home," he said.

"Thanks. So do you. But what I don't understand is why you live in a rental. And in an average neighborhood. Not that there's anything wrong with that. I was just…" She shrugged. "I was surprised. That's all."

"You aren't the only one in town making assumptions about me and my family solely based upon our last name."

"I'm sorry. It's not just assumptions, though. You're rich."

"I'm comfortable."

"That's what my wealthy clients say when they have a boatload of cash and property and don't want people to think they're show-offs."

"Maybe," he said. "But you're far from being poor, Sofia."

"No, not anymore. But I used to be." She tilted her glass and finished her drink. Then she shifted in her seat and studied him carefully. "I certainly didn't grow up in a family like yours."

"I had a good childhood—loving parents, travel, no financial worries. But it wasn't all sunshine and lollipops." He reached for the champagne bottle to refill their flutes.

She placed her hand over the rim of hers. "I'm okay for now. What was so bad about growing up 'Fortune'?"

He replenished his own glass and took a drink. "Even when I was a kid in elementary school, I had to vet my friends to make sure they weren't expecting more than friendship from me."

"That must have been tough. But welcome to being a woman."

"Good point." He downed his glass. "It seemed as if there was always someone in my life clamoring to get into my inner circle for social or financial reasons."

"That sounds terrible. I'll admit that was never a problem for me."

"I rolled with it when I was a kid. But in college, I had to be leery of who I dated." He didn't usually share stuff like that with people. Why was he opening up like that?

Sofiia reached for the bottle and poured a splash of champagne in her glass. Then she lifted it from the coffee table. Instead of drinking, she held it steady. "Chased around the quad by packs of gold-diggers?"

"Something like that." He chuckled. Then he stilled. For some reason, it was important that she understand. "When I was in college, I dated a woman named Gina. We hit it off, and things went okay for a while. She grew up at her daddy's country club and was an ace golfer. She dreamed of going pro."

"Seems like your type. The point…?"

There she went again. Typecasting him. "Come to find out, Gina was actually on the hunt for financial backers who'd support her while she was on the tour."

"So you broke up with her?"

Beau took another drink of champagne. "There was another reason. She had a competitive streak that sometimes got out of hand." Damn. The bubbly had sure loosened his lips.

"What's the matter, Mr. Fortune? Can't deal with a competitive woman? Too much to handle?"

"I can deal." He stole a glance at Sofia, but he didn't see any real similarity to Gina and her desire to win at all costs. "But it's exhausting to constantly be in a state of competition. And to feel used."

"Can't argue that." Sofia reached for the plate, took a strawberry and bit into it. "Hmm. These are yummy."

When she finished chewing, a chocolate smudge remained at the corner of her mouth. Unable to help himself, he reached over and wiped it away with his finger.

Her lips parted. "Did I make a mess?"

"No. You're fine." Their gazes locked, and something passed between them, something soul stirring and blood pumping.

Did she have any idea what that was doing to him? Before he could broach the subject, she stiffened and held up her glass. "I shouldn't be drinking this. I've probably had more than enough tonight." She got to her feet and placed her flute on the table, but she swayed.

Beau reached out to steady her with his free hand. Once she was more stable, he set his own glass beside hers and stood. "Are you okay?"

"I'm…not sure." She looked up at him, those big brown eyes zeroing in on him. "Are you?"

He'd had more than his share of champagne. And whether he had his car here or not, he'd definitely need to take an Uber home. But by the way she was gazing at him, she might be asking how he felt being so close to her, breathing in her light floral scent, watching those luscious lips, it was a different story. He'd completely lost his head.

"I'm not exactly okay," he said. "Right this minute, I'd like to kiss you again."

"Then, what are you waiting for?"

Not a damn thing.

Beau reached for Sofia's hand and drew her to her feet. The moment his lips touched hers, she lost herself in the warmth of his embrace and kissed him with a longing she hadn't expected. Her mouth opened, and his tongue sought hers. He tasted chocolaty sweet, and she couldn't seem to get enough of him.

The kiss deepened, and she leaned into him. Somewhere, in the far corner of her tipsy mind, she remembered telling herself not to get romantically involved with him. But oddly enough, whatever reason she'd had for making that decision escaped her.

As he trailed his fingertips along her cheek, she tingled at his touch. She couldn't keep her hands to herself, either. She relished the feel of him, of his broad chest, corded muscles.

Damn. She couldn't remember ever feeling this intensity, this urgency. They stroked, caressed and explored each other until she doubted either one of them could remain upright much longer—or fully clothed.

Beau drew back, breaking the kiss. Her breath caught, and her heart pounded out in primal need.

"Is something wrong?" she asked, her voice a mere whisper.

"Just a bit."

She didn't understand. He'd just kissed her as if there was no tomorrow—and no holding back.

He cupped her face with both hands, then blew out a ragged sigh. "That champagne is doing a real number on us, Sofia. And when we make love, I want us both to be fully present, sober and completely on board."

What the heck? Sofia was speechless. And annoyed. And embarrassed.

Sure, she was a little tipsy, but she wasn't drunk. She knew what she was doing, what she wanted. But she wasn't about to beg.

Instead, she stood tall and gathered her strength. "I think you'd better leave."

A part of her waited for him to object, but he slowly nodded his head. "You're right. Let's sleep on it."

He started for the door. She'd be damned if she'd stop him. Instead, she followed him, too stunned to speak. Too flustered. And hurt.

He brushed a quick kiss on her brow, then opened the door and let himself out. She stood in the entry for a moment and watched him pull his phone out of his pocket and scan the display. No doubt requesting the Uber. Then he started down the street.

Once he was out of sight, she locked the front door. She grabbed the bottle of champagne, nearly empty, and took it to the kitchen, but she stopped in her tracks when she spotted the two trophies on the counter—mocking her, it seemed. She swore under her breath, then reached for the dishtowel and draped it over them the best she could.

Then she poured the rest of the champagne down the sink and emptied the coffeepot, too. She didn't have need of either tonight. After turning off the lights in the main part of the house, she went to the bathroom.

By the time she'd washed her face, brushed her teeth, slipped into a nightie and gotten into bed, she was still stewing over what had gone down— and what might have happened.

She couldn't believe she'd almost gone to bed with Beau Fortune. She'd certainly been up for it—100 percent. But he'd had second thoughts.

She probably ought to thank him. Admittedly, no matter how embarrassed she was, she hadn't been sober or thinking clearly. She should've known better than to sleep with a business competitor.

And a Fortune at that!

As soon as the morning coffee finished perking, Sophia downed a half cup of the fresh brew. She was determined to put the whole Beau fiasco out of her mind, and a good workout ought to do the trick. So she slipped on a pair of yoga pants and a matching top.

She'd no more than put on her running shoes when her cell phone rang. She answered without looking at the display.

"How are you feeling?" Beau asked.

Embarrassed. Angry. Frustrated. She wasn't about to go there. Not with him. Not today. The last thing she wanted to admit was that she'd had too much to drink last night, even if they both knew that was true.

So she rustled up every ounce of her dignity and self-confidence and snapped out a retort. "I don't have a hangover, if that's what you mean." She did have a dull headache, though. But she'd be damned if she'd reveal that. "I'm fine."

"That's not what I meant. I was wondering how you felt about what almost happened last night."

Until he saved the day? "Just so we're both clear on this, last night was a mistake I won't be repeating."

"It wasn't a mistake. It's just that… I wanted to make sure you were in a good place when we decided to make love."

"I was in my right mind. How about you?" Hell, after all, she hadn't been drinking alone.

"You misunderstood," he said. "When we make love, Sofia, I want you to remember *everything*."

She did remember everything. The frustration, embarrassment. The fact that she'd almost complicated her life and jumped into another relationship without thinking it through. "You were right to put a stop to it. We're too mismatched for any kind of a relationship, other than one that's professional."

"Do you know what I think?" he asked. "I think you're scared of your own feelings."

"Ha. You, Mr. Fortune, have an inflated ego. You may think you know me, but you have no idea what I'm thinking or feeling."

"Something's going on," Beau said. "Are you still hung up on that guy you were dating?"

Patrick? "No." It had nothing to do with him. Or maybe it did. Right now, she had a lot to sort out. But there was one thing she did know. She was in flight mode.

"Can we talk about this later?" Beau asked. "In person. Maybe over lunch?"

"There's no need for that. Case closed. Anyway, I need to go. I have an early appointment this morning, and I don't want to be late." Then she ended the call, as well as any lingering thoughts about romance. They were too different, and it would never work out. She was done with Mr. Beau Fortune. *Adios!*

She grabbed her keys and headed out the door, anger and resentment simmering through her bloodstream. But in the midst of it all, a bit of grief dogged her all the way to the gym.

Beau stood in his bedroom, staring at the cell phone in his hand. Damn. Sofia had just hung up on him. Maybe not in a burst of anger, but she'd clearly been annoyed. He didn't need an oracle to tell him she planned to cut him out of her life.

He slowly shook his head. He'd tried to do the right thing last night, and she'd taken offense. He blew out a sigh, then walked to the living room, where Draper sat on the sofa, a cup of coffee in hand. The package that arrived last week sat on the lamp table next to him.

"What's up?" Draper asked. "You look like someone just kicked you to the curb."

Sofia pretty much had. But Beau wasn't going to talk over his problems with Mr. No-Commitments.

"It isn't that big of a deal," Beau said.

Draper appeared skeptical, but he didn't pry. Instead, he seemed to respect Beau's obvious attempt to steer the conversation in another direction and pointed to the package. "Is this the box you told me arrived the other day?"

Beau nodded. "That's it."

"I thought you said that box was for me. It's addressed to B. Fortune."

"I already looked at the address. There isn't an initial on it. That mark in front of Fortune is just a smudge of ink. Besides, I didn't order anything. It has to be yours."

"Yeah, well, I didn't order anything, either." Draper reached for the box and handed it to Beau. "Take another look at that smudge. It says B. Fortune."

Beau studied it. His brother was right. That smudge had once been an initial. "Okay, but what you're calling a *B* could just as easily be a *D*."

"Just go ahead and open it," Draper said, waving off his comment. "You won't know who sent it until you see what's inside."

Beau plopped down in the easy chair and ripped off the tape. Then he opened the flaps, looked inside and pulled out the white tissue paper. What the…?

He scrunched his brow and cocked his head. "What the heck is this?" He pulled out a pink blanket.

There had to be a mistake. He definitely hadn't ordered a blanket. Even if he had, he wouldn't have chosen that color. He pulled it out and unfolded it.

"Who sent you that?"

"I don't have a clue." It was way too small for a king-size bed. Hell, it was too small for a twin. Maybe it was some kind of throw.

Draper's brow furrowed. "Hey, let me see that."

"Gladly." Beau tossed it to him.

His brother studied it, then lifted a corner

and showed it to Beau. "Look at that. It's mono-grammed with an *F*."

An *F*? As in *Fortune*? "That makes no sense."

Still, it looked like an anonymous someone re-ally had sent a "present" to Beau. He shook the tissue paper, then looked into the empty box. No card. And without a return address, there was no way of knowing who.

"This has to be some kind of joke."

"Or maybe an old girlfriend insinuating that you fathered a baby girl."

No, that couldn't be. Beau had always been careful with the women he'd dated.

"It's not from any of *my* dates." He glanced again at the address label on the box, hoping to make out a *D*, to no avail. He grabbed the blanket and threw it on the sofa. "I'm just going to chalk this up as a practical joke."

In the meantime, he was going to pour himself a cup of coffee and stew about Sofia. What the heck was going on with her?

"Hey," Draper said. "I know you. Something's eating at you, and it's not a baby blanket."

Beau shrugged. "It's Sofia."

"Thought so. What'd you do?"

"It's what I didn't do. Take advantage of her. She was tipsy. We both were. And… Well. We kissed, but I knew she was running on alcohol and I was a close second."

"So, like the gentleman you are, you backed off. And now she's mad."

"That's it in a nutshell. I called her this morning, and she gave me the brush-off."

"She's embarrassed," Draper said. "And a woman scorned. Maybe she didn't want you to be a gentleman last night. But if you'd gone further, it would have been a dick move. And today she'd really hate you. Just let her cool off. She'll come around."

"You think so?"

"Yeah. You've got it bad for her, don't you?"

Beau shrugged again.

"Tell you what. Let's go play a round of golf and blow off some steam. What do you think? It'll give you a chance to check out the country club and form an opinion on joining."

"What the hell. Why not?" It beat sitting around the house on a Saturday, reliving that kiss and overthinking his decision and Sofia's reaction.

Let her cool off, Draper had said. *She'll come around.*

Beau hoped so. But Sofia wasn't like other women. And certainly not the type his brother dated. She was proud, strong and determined.

If she did come around, it wasn't going to happen overnight.

Chapter Thirteen

Sofia worked up a good sweat at the gym, but it didn't shake the regret that had dogged her all night long and now well into the morning. She'd had a lot to celebrate, but too much to drink and she hadn't been in full control last night. The alcohol had taken over her better judgment and caused her to forget a few important life lessons she'd learned the hard way.

Hearts could be broken by friends as well as lovers, and the only one she could really trust and rely upon was herself.

On top of that, it crushed her to think that Beau had come to his senses before she had.

Then again, she wasn't experienced or savvy when it came to dating. Her disappointing relationship with Patrick was proof of that. If she'd been smart, she wouldn't have gone out with him in the first place, but he'd charmed her with flowers and dinners at expensive restaurants. Sadly, she'd also been swayed by the fact that he had money and— unlike the first man she'd gotten involved with, James, from her college days—Patrick hadn't expected her to carry him financially. But Patrick's family wealth paled in comparison to Beau's. The Fortunes were in a whole different class.

And speaking of Beau's family, from what Sofia had gathered in news articles and magazine spreads, the Fortunes had their share of press. They were often generous to a fault, and some of them had a foundation that supported various charities and people in need. But not all of their news articles were good. There'd been fires, kidnappings and long-lost relatives showing up unexpectedly. The tabloids often went crazy with stories about them. So why take on any of the Fortune family baggage if she didn't need to?

Once back at home, she stepped into the shower. She relished the warm water as it pounded her skin and massaged her tense muscles, and she remained under the steamy spray longer than she needed to.

She'd no more than gotten out and grabbed a fluffy white bath towel when her cell phone rang.

Maybe it was Beau again. If it was, she'd let it roll over to voice mail. But when she snatched her cell from the bathroom counter, she realized it wasn't him. It was her mother.

She tapped the screen and took the call. "Hi, Mama. What's up?"

"You tell me, *mija*. Your *abuelita* and I have been pacing the floor all morning, just waiting for you to call. How did things go last night?"

Last night's fiasco wasn't up for discussion. "Everything went well," she lied. "Thanks for the strawberries and champagne. That was a nice treat."

"When we saw Beau driving your car, we thought…" Mama paused as if trying to choose her words carefully.

"I know what it looked like, but I'm afraid I did too much celebrating at the awards dinner, so Beau was nice enough to drive my car home. We munched on those delicious strawberries and had some more champagne. Then he took an Uber back to his house."

"Oh." Mama let out a sigh of resignation. "We'd hoped that…" She paused again. "I mean, we were just wondering if you made any further plans to celebrate. When are you going to see each other again?"

For a while, it had seemed that they were heading in that direction, but she'd nearly lost her head last night, and she couldn't let it happen again. She wasn't about to be swayed by her hormones and a rich, handsome guy she doubted she could trust.

"No, Mama. We don't have any plans." In fact, after last night, it was unlikely that they had a future at all. "I don't think I'm his type. And he isn't mine. I'm sorry to disappoint you."

"Oh, no. You've never disappointed us. I'm the one who should be sorry. Your *abuelita* and I jumped to conclusions, and we shouldn't have."

Sadly, Sofia had made that same jump last night. What a mistake that had been. Her ego was still stinging from what still felt like rejection.

"Your *abuelita* made a taco casserole for lunch. It will be ready soon. Why don't you come by and share it with us?"

"Sure." Sofia hadn't eaten very much at the dinner. And she'd thrown out the strawberries—a stupid move she blamed on a champagne buzz and wishing she'd tossed Beau out along with it. She'd also skipped breakfast this morning. So she was hungry—for a good home-cooked meal and for the unconditional love of Mama and Abuelita. "I'll be over as soon as I get dressed."

"Wonderful." Silence filled the line for a beat, then Mama said, "I'm sorry it didn't work out with you and Beau. But you know what they say. You have to kiss a lot of frogs before you find your prince."

"You're probably right." Apparently, Sofia still had a few toads to go.

She hadn't dated in high school because she'd been determined to study hard and land an academic scholarship. Even in college, after she'd been burned by James and her so-called BFF, she'd refused to spend the time, energy and emotion dealing with their betrayal. Instead, she became too focused on graduating with honors to develop much of a social life. And once she joined the work force, she'd been too busy building her client base and creating De Leon Financial Consulting to find a lot of time for romance. Too bad there wasn't an app for ways to develop a healthy social life. She'd jump on an investment like that.

But enough stewing about the past.

"I'll see you in a few minutes, Mama." Then she ended the call.

It wasn't a secret. Mama and Abuelita made it clear that they liked Beau and thought he and Sofia were an ideal match. But good looks, charm and an impressive bank account weren't indicators of one's character or honesty. And as far as Sofia was concerned, the jury was still out on Beau.

She could give it more time, she supposed, but she'd already recognized their differences. So her best bet was to forget about last night, pretend it never happened and get on with her life. Besides, she'd known all along. A relationship with Beau Fortune was merely a fleeting fantasy.

Maria had just pulled the casserole out of the oven when she heard the front door open and Sofia call out, "It's me. Lunch sure smells delicious. I hope it's ready. I'm starving."

There was nothing Maria loved more than preparing a delicious meal for her family and watching them enjoy it. "You're in luck, *mija*. I'm just about to put it on the table now."

Pepe, his fluffy white tail wagging, trotted into the kitchen, followed by Sofia.

"Where's Mama?" she asked.

"On the patio. She got a phone call and walked outside to talk privately."

"Oh, yeah? That doesn't sound like her. Who's she talking to?"

"Dan. I think they're making dinner plans."

Sofia grew somber, but Maria didn't address it. Her granddaughter had told her mother that everything went well last night. But that's not how her expression read.

"Is there anything I can do to help?" Sofia asked.

"You can take the salad out of the refrigerator. And fill the glasses with iced tea."

"All right."

The sliding door slid open and shut, as Camila

returned to the kitchen, her cell phone in hand, a smile stretched across her face. That smile faded as she studied Sofia. "What's wrong, honey?"

When Sofia didn't respond, Maria did it for her. "She's trying to keep up a brave front. Something went wrong last night, and she's not happy about it."

Sofia let out a sigh.

"I don't want to talk about it. I don't even want to think about it."

Moments later, when they were seated around the table, plates laden with food, Maria brought up the dreaded subject again. "I know you're not telling us the whole story, *mija*. If you get it off your chest, you'll feel better. And we might be able to help."

Sofia sucked in a deep breath, then slowly let it out. "This is hard for me to admit, but I had too much to drink at the awards dinner."

"That's not like you," Maria said.

"I mean, it's not like I guzzled a whole bottle of champagne by myself, but I hadn't eaten very much, and the alcohol went right to my head. That's why Beau drove me home."

Hmm. That was a gentlemanly thing for him to do. So far, Maria hadn't changed her mind about him. "Go on."

"When we got to my place, we opened the bot-

224 ANYONE BUT A FORTUNE

tle of champagne you left for me, and I had another glass."

Still, Maria couldn't see any reason to fault Beau.

"I got drunk. He kissed me, and I…" She paused and bit her lip. "I kissed him back."

Maria didn't see a problem there. "Was he a bad kisser?"

"No. It's just that the man throws me off balance."

"I take it the evening ended badly," Camila said.

"Beau took off so quickly that he left his Lone Star Best Award behind."

"Did he tell you why?" Maria asked.

"He said it was because we'd been drinking. And because we needed to be sober before…we went any further."

"Hmm." Maria leaned forward. "That sounds honorable to me."

"Maybe, but I might not have kissed him in the first place if I hadn't been tipsy. The alcohol lowered my inhibitions, and I nearly got involved with a man who isn't right for me. I've trusted my hormones before, that's a mistake I'll never make again."

"Don't be too quick to write him off," Maria said. "Take some time to think it over. Maybe, when you return his trophy, you can talk to him."

"No, I'm not going to worry about his trophy. I

don't think he even realizes he left it at my house. And since we were both recognized in what was actually a tie, he probably doesn't think his win was legit. Besides, he knows where it is. If he really wants it, he can come and get it."

Maria sat back in her chair. She'd had enough life experience to know when a man was interested in a woman. And when a woman was fighting her interest in him. "I like Beau, *mija*. I think you should give him a chance. You might change your mind about those differences. Just let things cool off for a while."

"Okay, I'll give it some time. But I'm not going to take that trophy to him. I'll mail it. Or better yet, I'll have my assistant drop it off at his office."

"In this case," Maria said, "I think it's best if you hang on to it for a while."

Sofia hadn't given her one reason to think that Beau was anything but a decent and honorable guy—and a true gentleman. So Maria was going to have to come up with a plan to get them back together.

And one had already begun to form.

Beau hoped that Sofia would realize he'd only been looking out for her best interests. Saturday went by quickly, thanks to the round of golf he played with Draper—but he didn't hear from her.

As Sunday dawned, he assumed she'd see reason and give him a call. But she didn't.

On Monday morning, he was tempted to make the first move, but he didn't want to push her. But by the time afternoon rolled around, his patience was worn thin. He'd always prided himself on being a man of action, but he didn't like the idea of showing up on her front porch uninvited. So he came up with an idea that would give him an opportunity to run into her "unexpectedly." And if that didn't work... Well, he didn't want to think about that.

He finished his last work email, then packed up his briefcase. On his way out, he poked his head inside his brother's office. "I'm leaving early, Draper. I'll see you later."

Once he got into his car, he called Dan and asked if it would be okay if he borrowed M.P. for a while.

"Sure. If you want him, he's all yours. What's up?"

"Sofia and I seem to have hit a roadblock. I've been waiting for her to call me, but she hasn't. So I thought I'd try to accidentally run into her at the park. But if I don't have a dog with me, I'm going to look desperate and needy."

"That's for sure. I feel your pain, man. I'm home now. Come and get him."

Not more than a half hour later, Beau and M.P. were on their way to the park. He'd timed his arrival so he'd have a good chance of seeing Sofia and Pepe.

Once he arrived, he unhooked the leash and let the dog run and play. Then he took a seat on a bench near the water fountain, prepared to sit there as long as it took.

He didn't have to wait long. Moments later, Pepe bounded across the lawn and ran right up to his furry friend. Beau's heart rate kicked up as he scanned the area, then it stalled when he realized Sofia hadn't brought her dog here today.

Disappointed yet hoping to get a few answers, he got to his feet and closed the distance between him and Sofia's grandmother.

"Good afternoon, Maria. It sure is a nice day." He nodded toward Pepe, who was playing a canine version of tag with M.P. "I see you have doggie duty."

"Sofia had to work late, and Camila went shopping." She cocked her head and gave him a once-over. "I see you're dog sitting again."

His plan had fizzled, but he mustered a smile. "Yes. Okay, you got me. I hoped I'd see Sofia."

"You did, huh?" Maria squinted as she looked up at him, then she used a hand to shield her eyes from the setting sun. She studied him carefully, as if trying to figure out his motive.

"Sofia and I had a little misunderstanding on Friday night, and I'd like to set things right."

A grin spread across her face, softening the age lines, and her eyes glimmered. "I'm glad to hear that. She's a good girl. I'm glad you're not giving up on her."

"It's a little hard to fight for someone who won't return your calls."

"Then you need to call again."

"I'm not going to chase her."

Maria slapped her hands on her hips. "What makes you so sure Sofia doesn't want to be caught?"

He stewed on the situation for a moment. Was Sofia rejecting him over his last name or his wealth? Maybe she just didn't like him. Crap. He hated not knowing where he stood.

Maria reached into her pocket and took out a piece of bacon. She gave a little whistle and called the dogs. They came running.

Too bad Beau couldn't tempt Sofia just as easily.

"I don't know what's wrong with your generation," Maria said. "You've lost that sense of romance. What you need to do is to make a grand gesture."

"Like what?"

"Flowers maybe. Chocolate? You're a smart guy. You'll figure it out."

He hoped so. But Sofia wasn't like other women, which was what he liked about her. And he didn't think flowers or chocolate would do the trick.

Chapter Fourteen

After work, Sofia stopped by her mother's place to get Pepe. When she entered the house, she found Mama in the living room, running a feather duster over the bookshelves.

She'd expected her dog to come running to greet her, like he always did, but he didn't. "Where's Pepe?"

"Your grandmother took him for a walk to the park," Mama said. "At least, that's what her note said."

"Nice." Sofia scanned the quiet living room. Two large shopping bags rested on the sofa. "What's all this? What'd you buy?"

She stopped dusting. "A few outfits. It's been so long since I had anything new."

And way too long since she'd had a date. Sofia smiled. Her mother was looking forward to going out with Dan. "Can I see what you bought?"

"Sure." Mama put down the duster, then pulled out a pair of black slacks, a colorful peasant-style blouse with puffy sleeves, along with jeans, a couple of blousy T-shirts and two pairs of sling-back, low heeled sandals.

"Wow. I love the shoes. Can I borrow them?"

"Perhaps. After I get a chance to wear them." Mama smiled, her cheeks rosy. "Dan's taking me to dinner tonight, and I want to look nice."

"I think you've already swept him off his feet."

"You might be right. Are you okay with that?"

"Of course. You're a big girl. He seems like *buena gente.* A good person."

Mama nodded, her eyes sparkling. She let out a soft giggle. "He makes me feel like a teenager. He called me last night, and we talked for over an hour. He's got a dry sense of humor, and it keeps me on my toes." She placed her hands on both sides of her face. "I smiled so much that my cheeks ached by the time we hung up."

"I'm glad to hear that. You deserve to be happy."

"So do you, *mija.*" Mama took a seat on the sofa. "I know you have your doubts about Beau."

Okay, this conversation was shifting into one

that made Sofia uncomfortable. She raised a hand to stop her mom from going any further. "It's okay."

Mom ignored the warning. "I think part of the reason is because of the way your last relationship ended. But you really should give Beau a chance. You might be surprised. I'm sure he's more sincere and trustworthy than Patrick was."

"I don't doubt that." Sofia reached for the discarded feather duster and ran it across the table's glass top. "I think my biggest problem is that I don't trust myself when it comes to choosing a decent guy. I'd rather not take the risk of ending up with the wrong man." She'd made that mistake twice already and she didn't like having to kick herself for missing the red flags. She set the duster aside and plopped down on the sofa.

Mama reached out and patted Sofia's knee. "True love is worth the risk. And, like I told you before, you'll never find your fellow unless you kiss a frog or two along the way."

"With my luck, I'll end up with no guy and warts on my lips."

Mama laughed. "That's an old wives' tale."

Before Sofia could respond, Mama's cell phone rang. When she looked at the screen, she brightened. "It's Dan."

Sofia could have sat there, listening in on one side of their conversation, but instead she got up and started running the duster over the TV console. As she went through the motions, doing a chore that Mama had already tackled, she thought back to the conversation she'd had with Beau— after they'd kissed.

Is something wrong? she'd asked.

Just a bit. When we make love, Sofia, I want both of us to be fully present, sober and completely on board.

She'd been embarrassed and defensive. But had she been wrong to take offense?

Even when he called the next day, she'd had her mind set.

I wanted to make sure you were in a good place when we decided to make love, he'd said. *When we make love, Sofia, I want you to remember* everything.

She blew out a sigh. Damn. Abuelita thought Beau had been looking out for her that night. And that he'd sounded honorable. But Sofia had been so locked into fear and romantic insecurity that she'd wanted to shut him out of her life before learning that she'd missed the signs and made another mistake.

But what if she'd woken up the next morning with a hangover and regrets for sleeping with the man snoring next to her?

Instead, Beau had saved her from that scenario. She let out a ragged sigh. She owed him an apology, she supposed. She also needed to return that Lone Star Best trophy.

She set the feather duster on the coffee table, then tapped Mama's leg. When her mother looked up, Sofia mouthed, "I'm taking off. I'll talk to you later."

Mama nodded, and Sofia headed out the door. Did she dare lay it on the line and tell Beau about her struggle, her concern about jumping into a relationship too soon, her fear of making another mistake? Either way, she had to go home. She'd left the trophy at her house, a terrible reminder of that bad ending to the evening, and the sooner it was out of sight, the better off she'd be.

With the trophy sitting on the passenger seat, Sofia drove to the house Beau shared with his brother and parked along the curb. Then she walked to the front door, the award in her arms, and rang the bell.

Draper greeted her with a charming smile. "Well, look who's here. Come on in. Beau will be home shortly."

She hesitated, feeling a bit skittish. "I just came to return this. Here." She handed him the trophy, and he set it on a table near the door.

"Thanks. But don't run off. I know he'll want to see you. Have a seat." He indicated the easy chair. "I was just getting ready to head out for the evening, but you're welcome to wait here for him. It won't be very long."

Sofia had the perfect excuse to leave—Beau wasn't home and Draper had to run. But the sooner she was able to talk to Beau and apologize, the better. "Are you sure?"

"Absolutely. Have a seat. Can I get you something to drink? Glass of wine?"

"No, I'm fine." Under the circumstances and considering the conversation they would need to have, liquid courage seemed like a very bad idea.

"If you'll excuse me," Draper said. "I need to get ready. But please. Make yourself at home."

Once Draper left the room, Sofia sat in the easy chair and scanned their bachelor pad. It still didn't strike her as the type of place where the brothers who ran Fortune Investments would live.

As her gaze moved to the sofa, something pink and draped over the backrest caught her eye. It looked like a woman's sweater. Or a small wrap of some kind.

Unable to help herself, she got up to take a closer look. She picked it up and frowned. That's weird. It was a hand-knitted baby blanket. And it was monogrammed. With an F.

For Fortune? What else could it stand for, especially here, in this house?

She didn't hear Draper return until he chuckled. "I told Beau it doesn't match the decor."

Her expression must have appeared confused, shocked or taken by complete surprise, because he laughed again and added, "It's not mine. Someone sent it to Beau."

The blanket grew hot in her hands. Was an old lover sending him a message of some kind? Her heart seemed to lurch. Was Beau a father?

"As a practical joke," Draper added with a wave of his hand.

That didn't compute. If someone sent a gift like that as a joke, there had to be some reason—either offbeat or sick—to think Beau would find it funny.

Sofia certainly didn't.

"Really, Sofia. It's a practical joke. Don't give it another thought."

"If you say so." But she wasn't buying it. She narrowed her eyes at the blanket.

Draper glanced at his Rolex watch. "Ah, look. I need to take off. But, please. Stay. He'll be here any minute."

"You know," Sofia said, pulling out her cell phone from her back pocket and pretending to read a text, "I forgot. I have something important to do." Something really pressing, like washing her hair or filing her nails.

She set the blanket on the sofa, draping it more evenly than she'd found it. She couldn't tell if it was new or barely used, but it didn't matter. This little pink blanket was a big red flag.

"I'll tell my brother you stopped by," Draper said. "He'll be sorry he missed you."

Yeah. Right. "Just let him know I returned the trophy." One last glance at the blanket, and Sofia sensed the situation with Beau just got a lot more complicated. She'd give him an opportunity to explain, but heck. Who needed this?

Sofia didn't wait for Draper to open the door. She let herself out, her hopes dashed, her heart taking a bigger hit than when Beau left her place on Friday night. But it was her own fault. She'd given him a pass way too soon. She should have trusted her initial instincts. Rumor had it Draper was a bit of a player. Apparently, Beau was, too.

She approached her car and slowed. Hey, wait. Maybe Beau had reason to be concerned about making love while intoxicated. What if a previous drunken encounter had resulted in a pink blanket?

It was certainly possible. Misfortune ran in the Fortune family. What made her think anything good could ever become of dating one of them?

Damn. Sofia might carry some baggage, but it appeared Beau had a moving van loaded with his.

Beau stopped by Dan's house to drop off M.P. and rang the bell. His buddy answered the door with a smile. "How'd it go? Did you run into her?"

"I'm afraid not. I did get a chance to chat with her grandmother for a bit while the dogs played.

So it wasn't a total waste." He'd barely handed over the dog's leash when his cell phone rang.

He wondered if it might be Sofia. Maria was probably home by now. Maybe she'd talked to her granddaughter on his behalf. But when he looked at the display, he spotted his brother's name. He glanced across the street. Draper's car wasn't in the driveway. He probably forgot to turn off the water or something.

"Hey," Beau said. "What's up?"

"You might have a problem, man."

Was it work-related? He assumed so. "What's wrong?"

"Sofia stopped by with our trophy and to talk to you a few minutes ago."

His pulse quickened. That didn't sound like a problem to Beau. It sounded more like good news. "And…?"

"She'd planned to wait at the house until you got home but then she saw that pink blanket on the sofa. I told her someone sent it to you as a practical joke, but by her demeanor and the look on her face, I don't think she thought it was the least bit funny." He cleared this throat. "Or a coincidence."

Beau raked a hand through his hair. Dammit. He should have stuffed it back in the box and dropped it off at the Salvation Army or the Goodwill or something. "Why didn't you say it was intended for you?"

"I didn't think that fast."

"What am I supposed to do now? She didn't want to talk to me before, so I doubt that blasted blanket is going to help."

"I don't have a flippin' clue. But I can tell you this. I'm happy to be single and unattached. Relationships are too much trouble."

"Tell me about it." Beau ended the call. His relationship with Sofia, if you could call it that, had been trouble from the start, but he wasn't sure how to fix it.

The way he saw it, he had three options. He could write Sofia off completely, go to the neighborhood pub, throw back a beer or two and play a couple of games of darts. Or he could drive to her house and talk to her face to face.

"Bad news?" Dan scratched M.P.'s neck, and the dog panted his approval. "Let me guess. More girl trouble?"

"Yeah."

"Well, kid, if she's the one, she's worth fighting for."

"Funny. Someone else recently told me that, too." And Sofia was worth fighting for.

He opted for a talk.

Ten minutes later, he arrived at her condo and knocked at the door. She answered, looking fresh, with her hair in a ponytail and wearing stylish workout clothes and white sneakers.

"Hey."

"Hey, yourself." But she didn't invite him in. So there was no use to make small talk.

"About that damned blanket," he said, "I don't know why someone would have sent it."

She stood her ground, using the door as a shield. "Could it be a past girlfriend?"

"I don't think so."

Her dark brow arched. "You don't *think* so?"

"Hey, look. I have a past. And so do you."

"True. But I don't have one with a baby."

"I don't, either."

"You just said you didn't know."

He crossed his arms and shifted his weight from one foot to the other. "I've always been careful. But you clearly don't believe me."

She shrugged. But she remained behind the door, relentlessly barring his entrance. "Did you ever stop to wonder why things like this happen to people in your family? Fires, kidnappings, long-lost relatives showing up unexpectedly? For Pete's sake, the Fortunes seem to multiply like bunnies."

"No more than any other family. It's just that my family is in the news while other families with problems stay in the shadows."

"Maybe. But count me out. I'm not going to be a part of the Fortune media circus."

"Dammit, Sofia. I don't have a baby. I'm sure

of that. But I have no freakin' clue who sent me
that blanket. Or why."

She tapped her fingers on the door. "A man
never knows for sure."

"Granted. But I'm responsible. I've always used
protection. So it's very, very unlikely. You'll have
to trust me on this."

She let out a hollow laugh. "Yeah. Right. Not
gonna happen."

A man could only take so much, and Beau had
just hit his limit. He wasn't going to beg or grovel.
But before he could even reconsider and give it one
last shot, she closed the door in his face, leaving
him standing on the front porch like a door-to-door
solar-panel salesman in Alaska.

Sofia spent an hour at the gym, but a workout
didn't help. Nor did it set her mind at ease. After
she got home and showered, she fixed herself a
cup of herbal tea. All the while, her sweet dog sat
at her feet, watching and waiting.

"Come on, Pepe. Sit outside with me." She
turned on the porch light, then slid open the door.
Once Pepe trotted outside, she shut the screen.

She pulled out one of two café-style, wrought
iron chairs that flanked a matching table.

The dog cocked his head as if trying to figure
out why she'd been so quiet this evening.

A pink baby blanket. Of all the crazy gifts.

Who'd send something like that to Beau as a joke? And if they had, why?

None of it made sense to her. She really needed to shake her anger. It's not like she and Beau were in a real relationship. She didn't have those kinds of feelings for him. What she felt for him was purely physical. And since he kept her on her toes mentally, there was an intellectual aspect to his appeal.

Taking a sip of tea, she decided to rethink the baby blanket. Instead of it signaling the end of the world, she'd look at it like a wake-up call.

"The last thing I need to do is get sidetracked at this point," she muttered to herself.

Whenever she let a man enter her life, things went sideways. Without that complication, she did great. She kept her head on straight, followed her unique business model and looked forward to the future.

Up until she found out Beau's last name, she'd been able to steer De Leon Financial Consulting into a successful company. And she wasn't biased. Even the Lone Star Best folks had seen and commended her for her business savvy and her vision.

But then he'd charmed her into thinking he was trustworthy.

Till the pink baby blanket.

"What is that supposed to mean?"

Pepe whimpered, then eased toward her and

placed his head in her lap. She ruffled his fur. "I don't have an answer, either."

But she wasn't going to stress about it. She didn't need the complication. No, Sofia was the kind of woman who was better off without a mate or a spouse.

"Men," she whispered into the night air. "Who needs 'em?"

Pepe whimpered again.

She reached down and lovingly rubbed his ear. "You're a good boy."

Apparently, Pepe was the only male she could trust.

Chapter Fifteen

Women. Who needed them?

Beau was about to throw up his hands in defeat, but instead, he tossed a load of shirts into the washer. He dropped a laundry pod into the drum and slammed the door shut. He'd given it his best shot, but there was no reasoning with Sofia. She didn't believe his explanation about anything. And certainly not about his reason for not making love with her on Friday night. Or his explanation about that blasted pink blanket. She'd assumed the worst about his old lovers and imagined a baby who didn't exist.

What else could he do?

He selected the correct settings on the washer and pressed Start. He supposed he could tell her she'd just have to trust him, but whenever anyone said something like that to Beau, it made him skeptical of their honesty and intentions. And he doubted Sofia was any different. But there were only so many long walks, hard workouts and cold showers a guy could take.

Yet in spite of his bravado, he couldn't shake visions of Sofia from his mind. Each night, when he closed his eyes, all he could see was her. He could even hear her laugh at a silly joke one of their students had told her or watch sympathy fill her eyes when talking to a teary-eyed teenage girl. He'd be back in the classroom, where he'd stand in awe of the way Sofia would guide the girl to the back of the room, where they could have a quiet chat—a pep talk, Sofia had called it.

Even now, when he thought about her, he could still smell the subtle scent of her floral perfume as she took him by the hand and led him to the middle of the gym. Damn, she'd rocked that red dress. In fact, whether she sported a business suit or a pair of yoga pants and an oversize T-shirt, she put other women to shame.

Needless to say, letting her go without a fight wasn't going to be an option. But if he didn't find a way to reach her, he was going to be in trouble. *Big* trouble.

The dryer alarm went off, and he opened the door, took out his jeans and started folding them.

He was tempted to open a beer, but when he entered the kitchen, his eyes landed on the coffeepot. Earlier this morning, he'd used the last of his favorite grind. So he'd better swing by Kirby's Perks to pick up another package.

Fifteen minutes later, he parked his car in front of one of the most popular shops in Rambling Rose and headed inside. He paused in the doorway and relished the aroma of fresh-ground coffee that mingled with the sweet scent of muffins and pastries.

"Hey, Mr. Fortune."

Beau scanned the tables and spotted a couple of the kids who'd taken his and Sofia's class, seated in the rear. Kelly Marshall grinned and waved him over to the table she shared with another girl and Jason Rhodes, the first baseman on the high school baseball team.

Beau returned her smile and moseyed over to them. "What're you guys up to?"

"Just having coffee," Jason said. "And putting the gift cards Ms. De Leon gave us to good use."

"Is she with you?" Kelly asked.

"No," Beau said. "Sorry, it's just me."

"That's cool." Kelly's hair was braided in multiple strands, and she tucked a long plait behind her ear, revealing four different piercings. "I just asked because I wanted to thank her for offering my sister an internship."

Jason sat back in his seat and rested his arm on the edge of the empty chair next to his. "It's weird that you're here alone. I mean, we're used to seeing you guys together. Is she going to join you?"

"No, I don't think so. She's…at work, I guess." Or at home. Maybe at the dog park. Damn, Beau couldn't go an hour without someone or something reminding him of her and making him wonder where she was or what she was doing. "She's been busy lately."

Jason grinned. "Too busy for a coffee break, huh?"

Sofia was definitely too busy for Beau, even though he figured she was making up things to do and finding ways to avoid talking to him. Or being with him. He still couldn't wrap his mind around it. Patrick, the ass, had really done a number on her, and now Beau was paying for her distrust of men.

Jason straightened, removed his arm from the chair and pulled it away from the table. "Have a seat."

Beau was about to say he couldn't stick around, that he was going to purchase the bag of coffee, then head home. But why rush? He didn't have anything else to do. "Sure. I'll just buy a cup of coffee, then sit with you guys for a while."

Moments later, with a pound of his favorite brew in a sack and a heat-resistant cup filled with the same, he returned to the kids' table with a plate of cookies and scones to share. Kelly introduced him to the dark-haired girl beside her, a junior named Sadie Choi, who lives in Rambling Rose Estates. Sadie wore her short hair tucked behind her ears, each of which was adorned with a good-size diamond stud.

Jason reached for a pastry. All the while, he eyed Beau carefully. "Something bothering you, Mr. Fortune? You seem kind of…stressed." He bit into a maple-nut scone.

No way. Beau's foul mood couldn't be that obvious. "Just another tough day at the office." In truth, though, the day had gone smoothly. At least, when it came to work. Too bad his personal life had hit a bump in the road.

"Know what I think?" Jason asked.

Hell, Beau was afraid to ask. He took a sip of coffee. "What's that?"

"I think you and Ms. De Leon were dating, and it didn't work out."

Beau tried to laugh it off, but he didn't have much luck. "What makes you think that?"

"Come on, man. We saw the way she looked at you when you were busy doing something else. And you did the same thing to her."

So she'd been stealing peeks at him, too? Nice to know, although that wasn't much help now.

"And then at the dance," Kelly said, breaking a chocolate chip cookie in half, "you guys looked like you belonged together."

Jason agreed, taking the other half of the cookie. Ah, to be that young and consume all those calories with no net impact on the gut. "So did you break up?"

Was the truth that apparent in his expression, his demeanor? Beau tore his gaze from Jason and studied the steam snaking up from his cup. But he couldn't lie, even if he ought to. "She and I were kind of dating, but she decided to end things."

"What'd you do?" Jason asked.

Beau hadn't done anything. At least, not in his mind's eye.

Kelly elbowed Jason. "Dude, don't be rude. It's none of your business why they split. If he wants you to know, he'll tell you."

Jason sobered. "Sorry, man. I was just trying to help."

"No offense taken." The sad thing was, Beau ought to keep the reason to himself, but he had no idea what to do or how to get through to Sofia. "I guess she thinks I owe her an apology."

"Then do it," Kelly said. "And make it a good one."

"I've got an idea," Jason said. "Things looked

pretty awesome between you guys on the night of the dance. I think a little eighties music might get to her."

"Or better yet," Kelly said, "how about taking an idea from one of the movies. You could do something romantic but remind her of how she was feeling at the dance."

"Yeah," Jason said. "You could reach for her hand and say, 'Nobody puts Sofia in the corner.'"

Beau couldn't help but smile at Patrick Swayze's famous line in *Dirty Dancing*. But no. He didn't think that would do the trick. Sofia wasn't likely to be moved by something that simple.

"I got it!" Jason broke into a bright-eyed grin. "You should stand outside her window, holding a boom box and playing 'In Your Eyes,' by Peter Gabriel. Just like John Cusack did in *Say Anything*."

"Ooh," Kelly said. "I love that. But don't play that song. You need to play 'The Lady in Red' by Chris De Burgh. That would remind her of how she felt slow dancing with you."

Beau must be losing it, because that suggestion sounded kind of cool. Besides, Maria had said he needed "a grand gesture." Maybe the kids were on to something.

"Listen, guys. I've got to run." He had a lot to think about and consider. "But thanks for your advice."

"I hope you take it," Kelly said. "She'll love it, Mr. Fortune."

Beau gave her a noncommittal wink. "I'll see you around."

Deep inside, his gut told him that Sofia felt something for him, too. After all, she'd stopped by to return the Lone Star Best trophy, so that had to mean she'd begun to see reason.

Beau reached for the door, then stopped dead in his tracks. He turned around. "Say, guys. You didn't send me a pink blanket as a joke, did you?"

From the confused look on their young faces, he figured it wasn't them. But who was it?

As he walked out into the warm, afternoon sun toward his car, he shook off his curiosity. He had a grand gesture to plan.

The sun dipped low in the Texas sky, and daylight had dimmed as the De Leon women gathered together for their weekly family dinner. Sofia scanned the small backyard and the twinkly white lights that adorned the patio cover. A candle and a bottle of Chianti sat on the red-linen-draped table while Alexa played a variety of old Dean Martin hits in the background.

"I thought I'd change things up tonight," Abuelita said, delivering a vegetarian antipasto salad.

Mama sat down and spread a linen napkin over

her lap. "It's a lovely evening. It's nice to eat outside for a change."

Sofia had to agree, but the setting and the romantic mood was hard to ignore. All they needed was a moon the size of a big pizza pie.

"Mija," Abuelita said, "you haven't touched a bite. Aren't you hungry?"

"I love Italian food," Sofia said. "And I really enjoy being with you. I'm also glad that I don't have to cook on Wednesday nights, but honestly, I've kind of lost my appetite."

"Are you troubled about Beau?" Abuelita set down her fork. "I'd hoped tonight's setting would make you realize what you're missing out on."

Sofia sighed and all but rolled her eyes. "I figured you were up to something with the candles, music and wine. But I'm afraid it's having an opposite effect on me."

"Have you talked to Beau yet?" Mama asked.

"I was going to, but now I don't want to talk to him at all."

"I don't understand." Worry lines furrowed Mama's brow. "Have you seen a side to him that we haven't?"

"What's wrong with him?" Abuelita asked.

"Besides the fact that he's a Fortune and his family has more money than Fort Knox, not to mention they have more drama than the paparazzi can handle?"

Abuelita waved her off and clicked her tongue. "And you're the granddaughter of immigrants. How does that affect your character?"

"It's definitely affected who I am—my work ethic, for one thing. And it's affected my opinion that people who never have to work and who can rely on their family's name to get ahead have a lot to prove to me."

"So, Beau hasn't proven himself yet?" Mama asked.

"I was beginning to think he had." Sofia lifted her napkin and blotted her lips. "But just so you know, the last time you both coached me regarding my love life—or the lack thereof—I reconsidered my romantic fiasco last Friday night and realized you had a point. So I dropped by Beau's house to return his trophy. I had every intention of apologizing and suggesting that we start over and take things slow and easy."

Abuelita leaned forward and lifted her brow. "And?"

Sofia blew out a sigh. She poured herself a glass of wine, then told them about the baby blanket and Beau's explanation for it. "So, you see, he clearly has a complicated life. And I don't want to get involved with another man I can't trust."

Abuelita sat back in her seat. "I had a big plan to bring you two together, but I guess it's not going to work. *Que lastima.*"

"I don't understand," Mama said. "He told you it was a practical joke. And that he doesn't know anything about a child he might be responsible for. Why can't you believe him?"

"Why should I?" Sofia took her fork, speared a meatball and studied it a moment.

"Has he ever lied to you before?" Abuelita asked.

"No." At least, not that Sofia was aware of.

Damn. They were tag-teaming her. And she didn't like the line of questioning. Or her answers.

"Has he taken advantage of you in any way?" Mama asked.

Sofia's cheeks warmed at the memory of that night. "No."

Mama shook her head. "So you shut him out for no good reason. That must have hurt his feelings."

Sofia's stomach churned, and she set down the meatball she'd skewered, along with her fork. "I thought I had reasons."

Abuelita refilled their wine glasses. "If you're waiting for the perfect man to pop into your life, you might as well get yourself a cat and a romance novel. Everyone wants the perfect partner. But perfect people don't exist."

"I suppose you're right."

"I loved your grandfather more than anything in this world," Abuelita said. "And when he died, I knew there'd never be another man who could take his place in my heart. But my Carlos was human. And he had flaws. We all do. You included."

Sofia set aside her plate of spaghetti. It was no use even trying to eat.

"Mija," Mama said, "What's your deal breaker?"

"My what?"

"What can't you accept in a man?"

"Dishonesty. A lack of loyalty." Sofia shrugged. "Cheating on me." Like Patrick had done. "So that brings me back to that darned blanket."

"Oh, for goodness' sake, *mija*." Abuelita threw up her hands. "He told you it was a practical joke, and even if he did have a child out there, it was long before he met you. At least nine months. Right?"

"I suppose."

"From what I've seen," Mama said, "he's been bending over backward to be good to you."

Sofia had to admit her mother had a point. "And I kept shooting him down."

"That's okay," Mama said. "As long as you want him out of your life."

"Is that what you really want?" Abuelita asked. "To shut him out? For good?"

"I'm not sure. Probably not." A wave of dread washed over her. Had she pushed him away one too many times? "I'm not sure he'll give *me* another chance. Not after the way I treated him lately."

Mama reached over and placed her hand on top

of Sofia's. "Set your competitive streak and your ego aside. Give him the benefit of the doubt. Prove to him you trust him."

Her mother was right. But it wasn't that easy. "I've made such a mess of things that I have no idea how to fix them."

Abuelita brightened. "Maybe you need a grand gesture."

"Oh, come on. That's not my style." Sofia lifted her glass and took a sip of Chianti.

Yet the more she thought of Beau—the way he'd walked away from Patrick's drama at the Valentine's party…the way he'd refused to make love when they'd been drinking and she wasn't quite herself…

Damn. Maybe Mama and Abuelita were right. She needed to give him a big-ass apology. And, somehow, she'd have to prove to him that she trusted him with her heart. Only trouble was, she had no idea where to start.

Beau popped the cap on an ice cold beer, carried it to the living room and kicked off his shoes. He'd just plopped down on the easy chair and reached for the TV remote when Draper opened the front door and entered the house holding his gym bag. He'd shed the business attire he'd worn earlier for a pair of running shorts and a sweaty gray T-shirt.

"Good workout?" Beau asked.

"Just the usual."

Beau lifted his longneck bottle. "You up for a beer?"

"No, I'd better not. I need to take a quick shower and grab a change of clothes for tomorrow. Then I've got a date. How about you? Do you have plans for tonight?"

"Nope. Just beer and a movie." Anything to take his mind off his troubles.

"You still stewing over Sofia?" Draper asked.

Beau chuffed. "Yeah. I've got it bad. I'm not sure what love feels like, but I've never felt this way about another woman. And she's got me completely gobsmacked."

"What are you going to do about it?"

"There's not much I can do." Beau let out a wry chuckle. "I ran into a couple of the students Sofia and I worked with at the high school. And they gave me their sound advice."

"Oh, yeah?" Draper laughed. "Pray tell, what did you suggest?"

Beau told him about the boom box idea. "I know it sounds kind of lame."

"It does. And even if I'd seen that movie, I'd feel the same way. Besides, where would you find a boom box anyway? Do they even make them anymore?"

"Actually," Beau said, "I saw one in the garage the other day. On a shelf."

"I have no idea how you managed to spot that. The Dobsons have stacked their stuff clear to the rafters. I'm surprised you can find anything in there. I was looking for an extension cord the other day, and when I opened the door, I decided it would be faster and easier to drive to the hardware store and buy one."

"I hear you." Beau let out a sigh.

"But back to your floundering love life," Draper said. "Teenagers don't know anything about women and romance. If you're looking for solid advice, you'd be better off taking it from a grown man, one who knows how to charm a lady."

"And I know just the guy, right?"

Draper grinned. "Yep. Take Sofia someplace nice and pull out all the stops—red roses, a limousine, fancy restaurant, violins…"

"That's way over-the-top for Sofia. She has a problem with the Fortune family wealth and fame. Not to mention what she calls the 'Fortune family baggage.'"

"Most women want our gold-plated baggage."

"Maybe that's why I like her so much. She doesn't."

Draper strode over to the sofa and picked up the pink blanket. "I take it this is part of the problem."

"Yeah."

"And you explained to her that this was a joke? Sent to you by who knows who?"

"Yeah."

"And what? She believed you?"

"Nope."

"Well, that's a problem. She doesn't trust you."

"I know. And I've always been fair and honest with her."

Draper wadded up the pink blanket and tossed it at him. The stupid thing hit Beau in the face and dropped into his lap. Beau clicked his tongue, grabbed the stupid thing and threw it on the floor, next to the shoes he'd been wearing.

"You probably ought to dump that in the trash," Draper said.

Maybe so. But as much as Beau would like to, he refused to buckle on principle alone. Why hide the evidence when a crime had never been committed?

Damn. He hadn't realized just how deep Sofia's trust issues ran. He really needed to face the fact that it was over between them.

He took a drink of beer, hoping to wash thoughts of Sofia away. Yet he couldn't get her out of his mind. His heart wouldn't let him. Sexual attraction aside, he admired her as a businesswoman and a teammate. He also had the utmost respect for all she'd accomplished.

Dammit. Admit it, Beau. He blew out a sigh and faced the truth. He was hopelessly in love with her. And he couldn't stand by and watch any future they might have together dissipate into obscurity because of a stupid blanket.

But how could he convince her that she was the one who set his heart on fire and challenged him in every good way?

Words alone wouldn't work. Heck, they hadn't yet.

The only advice he'd been given, the only thing that made sense and might work, had come from Sofia's grandmother. Unfortunately, he was having one hell of a time figuring out what kind of "grand gesture" he ought to make. He could buy her something, but money didn't impress her—especially his money. And that was sure to push her away even further.

After twenty minutes of pondering the dilemma without a feasible idea, Beau carried his empty beer bottle into the kitchen. As he tossed it into the recycling bin, his cell phone rang. He swiped his finger over the screen. "Hi, Dad. What's up?"

"I meant to call earlier, but I got tied up in a late-afternoon meeting. I've got great news."

Beau could sure use something positive to focus on. "Let's hear it."

"Sheila O'Leary from *Financial Journal* magazine called this afternoon and said she'd like to do a big spread on Fortune Investments, particularly the Rambling Rose branch and that program you did with the high school students. Guess some Instagram post about it went viral. I gave her your number. She's going to contact you in the morning and wants to set up an appointment to meet you there."

"Wow." Beau could hardly believe his ears. "That magazine has a huge readership, and she's their top journalist. The exposure and publicity will be invaluable."

"That's right. It's the sort of break money can't buy. Sheila especially liked the angle of a wealthy and successful executive from a top-notch firm taking the time to teach financial basics to high school students." Dad cleared his throat. "I need to go. Your mom and I have dinner plans. Call me tomorrow—after you've had a chance to talk to Sheila."

Beau felt like doing a happy dance around the kitchen. This was just the sort of publicity he and Draper hoped to get after winning the Lone Star Best. He stilled. *The kind that money couldn't buy.*

Suddenly, an idea formed, and Beau knew what to do.

Chapter Sixteen

Sofia couldn't believe the news. Sheila O'Leary from *Financial Journal* wanted to interview her—today. At the office of De Leon Financial Consulting. She could hardly contain her excitement. She glanced at the clock on the wall—2:56 p.m. Sheila would be arriving any minute.

The intercom dinged, indicating her executive assistant was on the line, so she answered quickly. "Yes, Sally."

"Ms. O'Leary is here to see you."

"Good. Send her in." Sofia got to her feet. She straightened her suit jacket, then walked to the door and opened it, just as Sally escorted a petite platinum-haired woman in her midfifties down the hall and to her office.

The journalist extended a hand, her nails freshly manicured. "I know how busy you are. So I appreciate your fitting me into your schedule today."

"My pleasure," Sofia said. "Please come in and have a seat. Can I get you some coffee? Tea maybe?"

"A glass of water would be nice. Thank you."

Sally, who'd remained in the doorway, said, "Be right back."

Moments later, Sheila was settled in one of two leather chairs in front of Sofia's desk. A glass of water sat before her, as well as a small tape recorder. "If you don't mind, I'd like to ask you a few questions about your early years, as well as your education, before focusing on De Leon Financial Consulting."

Sofia told her about her father's death and the so-called financial adviser who'd depleted the life insurance proceeds Mama had hoped to invest. She wrapped up her story by explaining why her firm catered to women.

"You truly are a success story," Sheila said. "I'm so glad Beau Fortune suggested I interview you instead of him. He was right. Our readers will really enjoy your journey to success."

"Wait." Sofia furrowed her brow. "*Beau* sent you here to interview me?"

"Yes. Initially I contacted him for an interview about that class you two provided for Rambling Rose High School. My niece had brought it to my attention. You know, kids and their social media postings. Anyway, Mr. Fortune provided me with the details of that, as well as the Lone Star Best Awards you both received, but he insisted his story was pedestrian, nothing special. I needed to talk to you. And he was right. You're an amazing woman."

"He said that, too?"

"Yes, he certainly did. He insisted that your road to success would be more impressive to our readers than his. And, after talking to you, I have to agree." Sheila got to her feet and collected her recorder. "Thank you again. Do send me photos of your mom and grandmother. They're a big part of your success, too. I'll have a professional photographer stop by your office next week to take pictures of you. I think you'll be pleased with the article."

"Thank you. I'm sure I will." Sofia followed Sheila to the door and opened it for her to let her out. As Sheila strode down the hall and into the lobby, Sofia leaned against the doorjamb, still amazed at what she'd learned. Beau had given up the opportunity every financial firm wanted— a spread in *Financial Journal*. That must have been a difficult sacrifice for him to make, and she doubted it was from a place of guilt.

It was his way of telling her he was sincere, that he could be trusted. And, quite possibly, that he truly cared about her and could come to love her someday.

Sofia smacked her forehead. And she'd almost thrown it away over some stupid blanket.

She closed her office door and paced in a circle. She needed to apologize. To tell him she wanted him to be in her life and, more than that, she would trust him going forward—completely.

But how? She stopped pacing. Of course. She needed to give him the "grand gesture" Abuelita had suggested. Although she wasn't sure what to do.

She supposed she could hire a limousine, surprise him at his house this evening and take him to a romantic dinner. Give him a watch, maybe. But those were things he could easily do or buy for himself. It wasn't special enough and wouldn't show her commitment to him.

She thought for a moment, then an idea began to form. She could give him something more valuable than a watch or dinner. Herself and her time. She'd ask Sally to clear her calendar and to cover for her. Then she'd surprise him at the house or the office. In a limo with flowers and champagne, of course. That is, if he still wanted her.

And just in case he did, she'd book a romantic Airbnb on a vineyard. Better yet, at the Mendoza

Winery. Yes. The one where that bottle of wine had come from. The Fortunes and the Mendozas were close—so much so, they often married each other. That would be a good way to show him that she wasn't afraid to meet his family.

She tapped her intercom. "Sally, I need your help."

So much for grand gestures. No matter how many strings Sally tried to pull, she couldn't book the limousine until tomorrow afternoon. And there weren't any rooms available at the Mendoza Winery until next weekend. But there was no way Sofia was going to wait another day to apologize to Beau and try to make things right between them.

Mama and Abuelita were having dinner with Dan this evening, so she'd picked up Pepe and taken him home. She thought about changing into something more comfortable, but decided against it. Her apology had waited long enough.

On the way to Beau's house, she stopped and purchased a bottle of wine to take with her. Given the time and circumstances, coming here tonight with a bottle of merlot and laying her heart on the line was about as grand of a gesture as Sofia could make.

When she arrived, she spotted Beau's car in the driveway but not Draper's.

"Oh, good," she muttered. The last thing she needed when she told Beau what she'd come to say was an audience.

She pulled along the curb and parked, then with the porch light guiding her steps, she walked to the front door and rang the bell.

Moments later, Beau answered. When he spotted her on the stoop, his brow furrowed, his eyes wary. "Sofia…"

Clearly, he hadn't expected to see her here. Tonight. Good.

"I didn't…" He paused.

"I know." Her gaze lowered and rose up again, from his bare feet, a pair of black sweatpants and a white T-shirt revealing a trim belly, to his broad chest and muscular biceps and then back to his eyes. Her heart thumped and her breath caught. In an attempt to recover her senses, she lifted the bottle of wine.

"What's that?" he asked.

"A peace offering. And a gift of appreciation. I'd like to talk to you. Can I come in?"

"Yes. Of course." He stepped aside, allowing her into the living room, where an action flick was playing on the television, guns blasting, helicopters roaring. The TV remote, his cell phone and an empty bowl that appeared to have held chocolate ice cream rested on the coffee table.

After closing the door, Beau snatched the remote and turned off the television. "Have a seat."

Sofia glanced across the small room at the easy chair, where the pink blanket lay on the floor. Instead of sitting down, she set the wine on the coffee table, strode to the blanket, stooped and picked it up.

Beau let out a sigh that sounded defeated. "Look," he said, his voice sad, but not angry. "I told you about that, and I have nothing to add."

"Yes, I know. And I didn't believe you." She sucked in a deep, fortifying breath, then slowly let it out. "I'm sorry. I should have."

He merely gazed at her, his expression neutral. Obviously, he wasn't going to make this easy on her. And she could hardly blame him.

"How did the interview go?" he asked.

"Fantastic. Thank you so much. It was a generous thing for you to do." She reached for the bottle of wine and lifted it. "I just…well, I wanted to say thank you, and that I really appreciate what you did."

"Is that why you're here, bringing wine?"

"Yes." She bit down on her bottom lip. "And to serve up some humble pie to go with it."

His eyebrows raised. "Go on."

"I continued to point out how easy you have it. But I know that's not true. And just because I was raised in a home that was always strapped financially doesn't make me better than you. I'm sorry if I gave you that impression."

He folded his arms across his chest. "Yes, you did."

She nodded, realizing what a pain in the ass she must have been. And feeling both guilty and contrite. "I guess that's because…" She hesitated for a moment, then pushed through the rest of her apprehension. "I was afraid."

His brow furrowed. "Afraid of what?"

She fingered the edge of the blanket, then pressed on. "It was an old fear. And one that I never quite kicked. I was afraid to let down my walls and trust you."

"Are you still afraid?"

"Maybe. A little. I'm working on it, okay? And, for what it's worth, I'm going to work very hard."

His hands dropped to his sides, and he took a step toward her. "I'd never lie to you. And I won't give you a reason to ever doubt me. Understand?"

"Yes, and I believe you now." She shrugged. "I was wrong, and I don't know what else to say, other than I'm sorry. I was going to tell you this the other day, but when I saw the blanket on your sofa, it reminded me that you have a past I'm not aware of. And that you could have baggage I hadn't anticipated." She glanced down at her shoes, a pair of black high heels. Expensive. Stylish. Something a successful CEO would wear to the office. But on the inside, she was still that little girl who had to constantly prove herself, as well as a woman who struggled to trust people because she'd been hurt. She looked back at him. "I've got baggage, too."

He nodded. "Of course you do. We all carry

some. But why should my baggage carry more weight than yours?"

"What do you mean?"

"For some reason, maybe because of the jerk you once dated—"

"Jerks," she said. "Plural."

"Or because you grew up in modest circumstances compared to me—you feel a need to work your ass off and prove yourself. But you don't have to prove anything to me. I don't see the need for us to be competitors, even in business. Believe it or not, Sofia, I've always considered us to be on equal footing. We're both top in our field. Aren't we?"

"That's where I had my doubts."

"Well, stop that. You're one of the most independent women I've ever met. But listen. You don't need to prove anything to me or to anyone. You're beautiful, brilliant and a dynamo when it comes to your business savvy. And you're right in that I've never wanted for anything my entire life. It really helped me to realize that. But believe it not, I've never needed or wanted anything until I met you."

"And then I screwed it up." She shook the blanket at him. "I'm such a fool."

Beau closed the distance between them. "Let's just say you put the brakes on while we both sorted through what we were feeling." His grin sparked her heart—and her faith in his sincerity.

"Can you forgive me for being a slow learner when it comes to relationships?"

"In a nanosecond."

A smile finally broke free and spread across her lips, while her eyes grew misty. "Oh, Beau. You're amazing. I don't know why I tried so hard not to believe it."

"Does that mean you might come to trust me? And love me?"

"I already do."

He snatched the blanket from her and tossed it across the room. "That's all I needed to hear. Come here, you." He took her in his arms and lowered his mouth to hers.

The moment Sofia's lips touched his, Beau kissed her with an insatiable longing he'd never felt before. She must be feeling it, too, because she leaned into him and opened her mouth. His tongue sought hers, dipping, and swirling and mating. He couldn't seem to get enough of her taste— or enough of her. He'd had other lovers, but he'd never experienced this kind of burning desire. Nor had he felt the compulsion to take a woman to bed and claim her as his—forever.

Their bodies fit together as if they'd been made for each other, two separate parts completing a perfect puzzle. He continued to stroke her, caressing her as he explored every inch of her silky skin and luscious body.

When he reached her breast, his thumb skimmed across the taut nub of her nipple, and her breath caught. He wasn't sure where this heated kiss was going—but he knew where he wanted it to go.

He drew his mouth from hers, his breath ragged. "Should we go to my bedroom? We might be more comfortable there."

She looked up at him and smiled. "There's nothing I'd like better."

Beau reached for her hand and led her down the hall to his room. If their kisses meant anything at all, making love was going to be magical.

As they stood beside his king-size bed, he drew her back into his arms and kissed her again—long and deep. As his hands slid along the curve of her back and down the slope of her derriere, a surge of heat and desire shot right through him. He pulled her hips forward, against his erection, and let her know how badly he wanted her.

She whimpered softly, then arched forward, pressing herself against him, revealing her own need, her own arousal.

When he thought he would die from sheer want and need, she ended the kiss and took a step back. Then she slowly removed her pale blue blouse and dropped it to the floor. He watched as she unbuttoned her black slacks and slid the zipper down in a slow and deliberate fashion. Her gaze never left his as she peeled the fabric over her hips and down her legs. Then she kicked them aside.

When she stood before him in a white lacy bra and matching panties, he swallowed hard, amazed at his good fortune. Her body, long and lithe, was everything he'd imagined it to be and more.

Following her lead, he peeled off his T-shirt, then the rest of his clothes, leaving no barriers between him and the woman he loved.

He eased toward her, arms open.

She skimmed her nails across his chest, sending a shiver through his veins and a rush of heat barreling through his blood. Next she unsnapped her bra and freed her full, round breasts, dusky brown tips peaked and begging to be fondled and adored.

He knelt before her. He cupped her breast and took a nipple in his mouth, lavishing one first and then the other. Fully aroused, she swayed and gripped his shoulders to keep her balance, her nails pressing into his back.

Unable to wait much longer, he lifted her in his arms and placed her on top of the bed. Her long, dark hair splayed upon the white pillow sham as her body stretched out on the matching comforter.

He paused for a beat, drinking in the angelic sight. "You're beautiful, Sofia."

A slow smile stretched across her lips. "So are you."

He got onto the bed, where they continued to kiss, to taste, to stroke each other until they were both breathless and drowning in need.

Beau didn't want to prolong the foreplay any longer, but he paused long enough to remove a condom from the unopened box he kept in his nightstand. After he'd protected them both, he kissed her again, hovering over her until she reached for his erection and guided him…home. And right where he needed to be.

He entered her slowly at first, then pushed deep. Her body responded to his, arching up to meet each of his thrusts, in and out, taking and giving, sharing the ultimate pleasure.

As Sofia reached a peak, she cried out and let go in a gripping climax. He shuddered and released along with her, in a sexual burst that left him seeing a swirl of spinning stars and believing in the miracle of love.

They held on to each other in an amazing afterglow that seemed to go on forever.

After a while, she said, "Are you able to take some vacation time?"

At that, he perked up. "Sure. Can you?"

"Yes, I already put it on my calendar at the office. I just hoped you'd be free, too. I'd like to kidnap you for a few days."

"I'd love that. What do you have in mind?"

"It's a surprise. And it's what Abuelita would call a grand gesture."

Beau laughed. "I love your grandmother. And your mom."

"Good. They feel the same about you." Then she slowly pulled away.

"Where are you going?"

"I need to go home."

"No you don't. Stay."

She smiled. "Believe me, there's nothing I'd like more. But I left Pepe home alone."

As she climbed out and reached for her clothes, he sat up in bed. "I don't suppose you'd want me to follow you home."

She turned to him and brightened. "I'd love that."

He slid out, too. "Then, what are we waiting for?"

Maria had forgotten to close the shutters tight last night, and the morning sun light peered through the open slots, waking her earlier than usual. Sofia would be bringing Pepe soon. So she took a quick shower.

Ten minutes later, she was dressed and ready to start the day. She glanced at the clock on the bureau. "Hmm. That's odd." Sofia must be running late.

She entered the kitchen, where Camila was putting on a pot of coffee.

"I'm going to walk over to Sofia's house and get Pepe," she said. "It'll save her a little time."

Camila turned and smiled. "That's nice. The coffee will be ready by the time you get back."

Maria made the short walk to Sofia's condo, where a car was parked along the curb. It looked familiar. Did her granddaughter have company? That didn't seem likely.

She gave a brief knock at the door, then, as she usually did, she let herself into the living room. "*Mija*, it's me. I thought I'd do you a favor and pick up Pepe."

At the sound of his name, the sweet dog came dashing from the kitchen and greeted her with a happy yip and a wagging tail. Maria bent to give him a scratch behind the ear. *"Aw, precioso. Donde esta Sofia?"*

"I, uh, I'm in the kitchen," Sofia called out.

Hmm. Her busy granddaughter rarely ate breakfast, especially if she was going to be late to the office. Was she sick?

Maria made her way into the kitchen, where Sofia sat at the table, across from Beau.

A slow smile stretched across Maria's face. "Good morning. I didn't expect to see you here, Beau. And so early." She winked. "It looks like you two worked things out between you. I'm glad."

Sofia, her cheeks rosy, got to her feet. "Would

you believe Beau stopped by to surprise me this morning? I thought I'd go in to the office late so we could have breakfast together."

Maria glanced at the handsome young man, his hair damp from the shower. A quick peek under the table revealed his bare feet.

Uh-huh. Maria raised her eyebrows and looked from Sofia to Beau.

He set aside his coffee mug, scooted back his chair and stood. "I know what this might look like, but Maria, I love your granddaughter."

Maria clapped her hands. "I knew it all along. You two belong together."

"You won't get any arguments from me," Beau said. "Is it okay if I call you Abuelita, too?"

"Of course, *hijo.*" Maria beamed. "I can't wait to run home and tell Camila."

Sofia lifted her index finger and wiggled it side to side. "Don't you dare, Abuelita. I know you enjoy being the bearer of good news in our family, but Beau and I want to tell Mama ourselves."

"Oh, of course. I suppose you're right." But that didn't mean Maria would keep the good news to herself. She couldn't wait to tell the neighborhood and the whole world that Sofia had found her own Carlos. Life didn't get any better than that.

Draper chuckled and slowly shook his head. "So you're really going to do it? On bended knee and all that?"

Beau reached into his pocket and withdrew a small black velvet box. "Got the ring right here."

Draper chuckled. "I hope she doesn't turn you down. I hate to see a grown man cry."

Beau winked. "She won't turn me down." At least, he was fairly confident she wouldn't. They'd had a great vacation, a whirlwind week of sharing, caring and lovemaking. "If you see anyone crying, those tears will be happy ones."

"Good to know. So does that mean you're moving out?"

"Not yet. I don't think her mother would appreciate knowing we were living together. At least, not until I make it official. But as far as you're concerned, I'm good as gone."

"Well, when you go, don't forget to take that pink blanket with you."

"Forget it. That blanket looks nice right where I left it. And it matches your decor."

"Like hell it does." Draper laughed. "So when are you gonna ask her?"

"Tonight. She's coming over for a drink."

"You know," Draper said. "I've got an idea. Let's invite your future in-laws to another barbecue at our house. There aren't any rain clouds on the horizon."

"Are you sure about that?" Beau asked. "Seems like a lot of work—and not much time to prepare for it. Why don't I take us all out to dinner instead?

How about the Mendoza Winery? I'll call and get a private room."

"No," Draper said. "Don't do that. Save that idea for an official engagement party. We'll keep things low-key and simple. Hosting Sofia's mother and grandmother at our place tonight will be a good way to introduce them to Belle and Jack. And who knows? Maybe Mom and Dad will fly out to meet their future daughter-in-law and her family."

"Good point. I like that idea."

Beau had been nervous all day. From time to time, he'd patted the ring box in his coat pocket as though it might have escaped. He didn't have any doubts about Sofia, and he doubted she had any about him. Still, tonight their lives would change forever.

Sofia arrived at the house at a quarter to six, just before her mother and grandmother, as well as Jack and Belle, were expected. Beau gave her a kiss, then led her to the living room, where they both took a seat on the sofa. On the coffee table, he had two crystal flutes and a bottle of champagne on ice. He poured them both a glass.

She slipped her hand into his. "Thank you for inviting us to dinner. Mama and Abuelita are looking forward to it. And they were thrilled to be included in the meal prep."

"Yeah, well it seems to me that the Fortunes and the De Leons will make a good team. But not quite as good as the one you and I have made. In fact, I'd like to propose a merger."

She shot him a quizzical glance. "A business merger?"

He released her hand, got up from the sofa and faced her. Then he took a knee and pulled the velvet box from his pocket. "Will you marry me?"

She blinked, and she placed a hand over her chest. "I—I…" Her lip quivered, and her eyes filled with tears.

He hoped they were happy ones. "I love you Sofia. And I enjoy every minute we're together. I think you feel the same way about me."

She nodded. "I do."

"So why wait?"

She studied his face, then glanced at the ring, which had cost a small fortune. But she was worth all that and so much more "I'm…speechless."

He got to his feet. "All you have to say is yes."

"Yes! Yes. Yes."

He opened his arms, and she stepped into his embrace.

"You may not be ready to set a wedding date, honey, but whenever you are, you won't hear any arguments from me. As far as I'm concerned, our partnership is one that will last a lifetime."

"I love you, Beau. This is…a wonderful surprise."

He took the velvet box from her hand and pulled

the ring free. "Will you wear it? And show the world how we feel about each other?"

She looked at him with a sense of wonder, then she took the ring and slipped it on her finger. She glanced at it for only a beat, then said, "I don't remember ever being this happy. I love you, Beau Fortune."

He laughed. "I'm glad, because I love you, too." He watched her study the sparkling ring on her finger.

"It's…beautiful."

"And so are you, honey. Maybe someday, we can expand our partnership and have a baby or two."

"A little girl?"

"Girl or boy. One of each. Or as many as you want."

She turned and reached for the pink baby blanket that was draped over the sofa. Using it as a rope, she slipped it around his waist and playfully drew him to her.

"Do you plan to wrap our babies in that thing?" he asked, chuckling.

"Why not?" Her eyes sparkled with mirth. "This blanket reminds me of our relationship— totally unexpected, a little quirky and somehow just right."

"I couldn't agree more." Then he kissed her, slow and sweet. A kiss with the promise of a bright and happy future.

When it ended, he said, "After we get married and start a family, we're going to need a bigger house."

"You're right," she said. "But please, not one at Rambling Rose Estates. I'm not part of the country club set."

"I know. Having a home there never crossed my mind. I'd rather buy some property and build the perfect home—one that reflects each of us."

Sofia smiled. "Don't forget that my family just multiplied tenfold or more. So it'll have to be large enough to host family holidays."

"Absolutely." He brushed a kiss on her brow. "And it will need to have a kitchen that Abuelita will approve of since I'd like her to feel free to cook for us whenever she wants to."

"I have a feeling Dan might be entering the picture, too. I've seen the way he looks at my mother."

"Me, too. I hope you see the same thing in my eyes—sincerity, respect and love."

Sofia's smile dimpled her cheeks. "Don't forget desire."

"Never." Then they kissed again, eager to see their future unfold.

A bright future together.

One that would last forever.

* * * * *

*Look for the next book in the new
Harlequin Special Edition continuity
The Fortunes of Texas: The Wedding Gift*

Cinderella Next Door
by Nancy Robards Thompson

*On sale April 2022 wherever Harlequin books
and ebooks are sold.*

*And catch up with the previous titles in
The Fortunes of Texas: The Wedding Gift:*
Their New Year's Beginning
by USA TODAY *bestselling author
Michelle Major*

A Soldier's Dare *by Jo McNally*

*Available now, wherever Harlequin books
and ebooks are sold.*

**WE HOPE YOU ENJOYED
THIS BOOK FROM**

Believe in love. Overcome obstacles. Find happiness.

Relate to finding comfort and strength in the
support of loved ones and enjoy the journey
no matter what life throws your way.

6 NEW BOOKS AVAILABLE EVERY MONTH!

HSEHALO2020

#2899 CINDERELLA NEXT DOOR

The Fortunes of Texas: The Wedding Gift
by Nancy Robards Thompson

High school teacher and aspiring artist Ginny Sanders knows she is not Draper Fortune's type. Content to admire her fabulous and flirty new neighbor from a distance, she is stunned when he asks her out. Draper is charmed by the sensitive teacher, but when he learns why she doesn't date, he must decide if he can be the man she needs...

#2900 HEIR TO THE RANCH

Dawson Family Ranch • by Melissa Senate

The more Gavin Dawson shirks his new role, the more irate Lily Gold gets. The very pregnant single mom-to-be is determined to make her new boss see the value in his late father's legacy—her livelihood and her home depend on it! But Gavin's plan to ignore his inheritance and Lily—*and* his growing attraction to her—is proving to be impossible...

#2901 CAPTIVATED BY THE COWGIRL

Match Made in Haven • by Brenda Harlen

Devin Blake is a natural loner, but when rancher Claire Lamontagne makes the first move, he finds himself wondering if he's as content as he thought he was. Is Devin ready to trade his solitary life for a future with the cowgirl tempting him to take a chance on love?

#2902 MORE THAN A TEMPORARY FAMILY

Furever Yours • by Marie Ferrarella

A visit with family was just what Josie Whitaker needed to put her marriage behind her. Horseback-riding lessons were an added bonus. But her instructor, Declan Hoyt, is dealing with his moody teenage niece. The divorced single mom knows just how to help and offers to teach Declan a thing or two about parenting—never expecting a romance to spark with the younger rancher!

#2903 LAST CHANCE ON MOONLIGHT RIDGE

Top Dog Dude Ranch • by Catherine Mann

Their love wasn't in doubt, but fertility issues and money problems have left Hollie and Jacob O'Brien's marriage in shambles. So once the spring wedding season at their Tennessee mountain ranch is over, they'll part ways. Until Jacob is inspired to romance Hollie and her long-buried maternal instincts are revived by four orphaned children visiting the ranch. Will their future together be resurrected, too?

#2904 AN UNEXPECTED COWBOY

Sutton's Place • by Shannon Stacey

Lone-wolf cowboy Irish is no stranger to long, lonely nights. But somehow Mallory Sutton tugs on his heartstrings. The feisty single mom is struggling to balance it all—and challenging Irish's perception of what he has to offer. But will their unexpected connection keep Irish in town...or end in heartbreak for Mallory and her kids?

YOU CAN FIND MORE INFORMATION ON UPCOMING HARLEQUIN TITLES, FREE EXCERPTS AND MORE AT HARLEQUIN.COM.

HSECNM0222

SPECIAL EXCERPT FROM

HQN

Mariella Jacob was one of the world's premier bridal designers. One viral PR disaster later, she's trying to get her torpedoed career back on track in small-town Magnolia, North Carolina. With a second-hand store and a new business venture helping her friends turn the Wildflower Inn into a wedding venue, Mariella is finally putting at least one mistake behind her. Until that mistake—in the glowering, handsome form of Alex Ralsten—moves to Magnolia too...

Read on for a sneak preview of
Wedding Season,
the next book in USA TODAY *bestselling author Michelle Major's Carolina Girls series!*

"You still don't belong here." Mariella crossed her arms over her chest, and Alex commanded himself not to notice her body, perfect as it was.

"That makes two of us, and yet here we are."

"I was here first," she muttered. He'd heard the argument before, but it didn't sway him.

"You're not running me off, Mariella. I needed a fresh start, and this is the place I've picked for my home."

"My plan was to leave the past behind me. You are a physical reminder of so many mistakes I've made."

"I can't say that upsets me too much," he lied. It didn't make sense, but he hated that he made her so uncomfortable. Hated even more that sometimes he'd purposely drive by her shop to get a glimpse of her through the picture window. Talk about a glutton for punishment.

She let out a low growl. "You are an infuriating man. Stubborn and callous. I don't even know if you have a heart."

"Funny." He kept his voice steady even as memories flooded him, making his head pound. "That's the rationale Amber gave me for why she cheated with your fiancé. My lack of emotions pushed her into his arms. What was his excuse?"

She looked out at the street for nearly a minute, and Alex wondered if she was even going to answer. He followed her gaze to the park across the street, situated in the center of the town. There were kids at the playground and several families walking dogs on the path that circled the perimeter. Magnolia was the perfect place to raise a family.

If a person had the heart to be that kind of a man—the type who married the woman he loved and set out to be a good husband and father. Alex wasn't cut out for a family, but he liked it in the small coastal town just the same.

"I was too committed to my job," she said suddenly and so quietly he almost missed it.

"Ironic since it was your job that introduced him to Amber."

"Yeah." She made a face. "This is what I'm talking about, Alex. A past I don't want to revisit."

"Then stay away from me, Mariella," he advised. "Because I'm not going anywhere."

"Then maybe I will," she said and walked away.

Don't miss
Wedding Season *by Michelle Major,*
available May 2022 wherever
HQN books and ebooks are sold.

HQNBooks.com

Copyright © 2022 by Michelle Major

Get 4 FREE REWARDS!

We'll send you 2 FREE Books plus 2 FREE Mystery Gifts.

FREE
Value Over
$20

Both the **Harlequin® Special Edition** and **Harlequin® Heartwarming™** series feature compelling novels filled with stories of love and strength where the bonds of friendship, family and community unite.

YES! Please send me 2 FREE novels from the Harlequin Special Edition or Harlequin Heartwarming series and my 2 FREE gifts (gifts are worth about $10 retail). After receiving them, if I don't wish to receive any more books, I can return the shipping statement marked "cancel." If I don't cancel, I will receive 6 brand-new Harlequin Special Edition books every month and be billed just $4.99 each in the U.S or $5.74 each in Canada, a savings of at least 17% off the cover price or 4 brand-new Harlequin Heartwarming Larger-Print books every month and be billed just $5.74 each in the U.S. or $6.24 each in Canada, a savings of at least 21% off the cover price. It's quite a bargain! Shipping and handling is just 50¢ per book in the U.S. and $1.25 per book in Canada.* I understand that accepting the 2 free books and gifts places me under no obligation to buy anything. I can always return a shipment and cancel at any time. The free books and gifts are mine to keep no matter what I decide.

Choose one: ☐ **Harlequin Special Edition**
(235/335 HDN GNMP)
☐ **Harlequin Heartwarming**
Larger-Print
(161/361 HDN GNPZ)

Name (please print)

Address   Apt. #

City   State/Province   Zip/Postal Code

Email: Please check this box ☐ if you would like to receive newsletters and promotional emails from Harlequin Enterprises ULC and its affiliates. You can unsubscribe anytime.

Mail to the Harlequin Reader Service:
IN U.S.A.: P.O. Box 1341, Buffalo, NY 14240-8531
IN CANADA: P.O. Box 603, Fort Erie, Ontario L2A 5X3

Want to try 2 free books from another series? Call **1-800-873-8635** or visit www.ReaderService.com.

*Terms and prices subject to change without notice. Prices do not include sales taxes, which will be charged (if applicable) based on your state or country of residence. Canadian residents will be charged applicable taxes. Offer not valid in Quebec. This offer is limited to one order per household. Books received may not be as shown. Not valid for current subscribers to the Harlequin Special Edition or Harlequin Heartwarming series. All orders subject to approval. Credit or debit balances in a customer's account(s) may be offset by any other outstanding balance owed by or to the customer. Please allow 4 to 6 weeks for delivery. Offer available while quantities last.

Your Privacy—Your information is being collected by Harlequin Enterprises ULC, operating as Harlequin Reader Service. For a complete summary of the information we collect, how we use this information and to whom it is disclosed, please visit our privacy notice located at corporate.harlequin.com/privacy-notice. From time to time we may also exchange your personal information with reputable third parties. If you wish to opt out of this sharing of your personal information, please visit readerservice.com/consumerschoice or call 1-800-873-8635. **Notice to California Residents**—Under California law, you have specific rights to control and access your data. For more information on these rights and how to exercise them, visit corporate.harlequin.com/california-privacy.

HSEHW22

Love Harlequin romance?

DISCOVER.

Be the first to find out about promotions,
news and exclusive content!

Facebook.com/HarlequinBooks

Twitter.com/HarlequinBooks

Instagram.com/HarlequinBooks

Pinterest.com/HarlequinBooks

YouTube.com/HarlequinBooks

ReaderService.com

EXPLORE.

Sign up for the Harlequin e-newsletter and
download a free book from any series at
TryHarlequin.com

CONNECT.

Join our Harlequin community to
share your thoughts and connect
with other romance readers!
Facebook.com/groups/HarlequinConnection

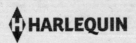

HSOCIAL2021